Sarah Morgan was born in Wiltshire and started writing at the age of eight when she produced an autobiography of her hamster.

At the age of 18 she travelled to London to train as a nurse in one of London's top teaching hospitals, and she describes what happened in those years as extremely happy and definitely censored!

She worked in a number of areas after she qualified, but her favourite was A&E where she found the work stimulating and fun. Nowhere else in the hospital environment did she encounter such good teamwork between doctors and nurses.

By now her interests had moved on from hamsters to men, and she started writing romance fiction.

Her first completed manuscript, written after the birth of her first child, was rejected by Mills & Boon but the comments were encouraging, so she tried again, and on the third attempt her manuscript *Worth the Risk* was accepted unchanged. She describes receiving the acceptance letter as one of the best moments of her life, after meeting her husband and having her two children.

Sarah still works part-time in a health-related industry and spends the rest of the time with her family trying to squeeze in writing whenever she can. She is an enthusiastic skier and walker and loves outdoor life.

THE BALFOUR LEGACY

A proud, powerful dynasty…

Scandal has rocked the core
of the infamous Balfour family…

Its glittering, gorgeous daughters
are in disgrace…

Banished from the Balfour mansion,
they're sent to the boldest,
most magnificent men in the world
to be wedded, bedded…and tamed!

*And so begins a scandalous saga of dazzling
glamour and passionate surrender*

8 addictive large print volumes

AUGUST 2010

Mia's Scandal by Michelle Reid
Kat's Pride by Sharon Kendrick

SEPTEMBER 2010

Emily's Innocence by India Grey
Sophie's Seduction by Kim Lawrence

OCTOBER 2010

Zoe's Lesson by Kate Hewitt
Annie's Secret by Carole Mortimer

NOVEMBER 2010

Bella's Disgrace by Sarah Morgan
Olivia's Awakening by Margaret Way

BELLA'S DISGRACE

Sarah Morgan

First published in Great Britain 2010
Large Print edition 2010
Harlequin Mills & Boon Limited,
Eton House, 18-24 Paradise Road, Richmond, Surrey TW9 1SR

© Harlequin Books S.A. 2010

Special thanks and acknowledgement are given to Sarah Morgan
for her contribution to *The Balfour Legacy* series.

ISBN: 978 0 263 21651 6

Harlequin Mills & Boon policy is to use papers that are natural,
renewable and recyclable products and made from wood grown in
sustainable forests. The logging and manufacturing process conform
to the legal environmental regulations of the country of origin.

Printed and bound in Great Britain
by CPI Antony Rowe, Chippenham, Wiltshire

CHAPTER ONE

SAND, sand and more sand.

Her father couldn't have sent her to a more remote place if he'd put her in a rocket and sent her to the moon. And if that had been possible, no doubt he would have signed the cheque, Bella thought bitterly as she curled her bare toes into the coarse sand of the desert and stared across the stark landscape. Come to think of it, this might as well be the moon. Or maybe Mars. The red planet.

Why a retreat in the middle of the desert?

Why not a nice spa on Fifth Avenue?

'Bella?'

Hearing her name, Bella gave a moan of despair. Already? It was barely daylight.

Reluctantly, she turned. *None of this was his fault*, she reminded herself. *It wasn't fair to take her anger and frustration out on him.* 'Early start, Atif?'

He was dressed simply in a white robe, the fabric

glaring under the beginnings of the Arabian sun. 'I meditate before dawn.'

Bella suppressed a yawn. 'Personally I prefer to start my day with a strong black coffee.'

'You can find a better start to the day by feasting on what lies around you,' the old man murmured. 'There's nothing as calming as watching the sunrise in the desert. Don't you find the peace soothing?'

'Honestly? It's driving me stark-staring nuts.' Without thinking, Bella reached for her phone and then remembered that it had been confiscated, along with everything else that she needed to communicate with the outside world. She tapped her empty palm impatiently against her thigh and then looked down at her fingernails with distaste. Given the choice between a coffee and a manicure, she would have opted for the manicure. 'Do you actually own this place?'

'I am merely passing through. When I am ready, I will move on.'

'I would have moved on after two minutes given the chance! I've been here for two weeks and it feels like a life sentence.'

How could her father do this to her? Thanks to him, she'd been cut off from everyone. *Left alone at a time when she desperately needed human comfort.*

The shocking discovery she'd made only two weeks earlier had left her numb and emotionally drained. The person she'd been before that night had gone forever. So had the naive assumptions she'd nurtured throughout her life.

Regret tore through her

You shouldn't have looked, Bella.

Like Pandora, she'd lifted the lid of the box and now she was paying the price.

'You allow emotion to grip you the way a falcon grips its prey.' Atif watched her with the same tranquil expression he adopted during their sessions together. 'You are angry, but your father sent you here for your own benefit.'

'He sent me here as a punishment because I embarrassed him.' Bella wrapped her arms around herself and wondered how she could feel cold in such a hot, oppressive place. 'I've embarrassed the whole family. Brought the Balfour name into disrepute. Again.' But no one had considered what the whole sordid incident had done to *her.* And the fact that no one had considered her feelings simply increased her sense of abandonment.

Remembering everything that had happened on the night of the Balfour Ball, Bella felt a lump build in her throat. She wanted to know how her sister Olivia was feeling about the whole thing— *she wanted to make amends.*

Her behaviour had been bad—she knew that. But she'd been goaded. Upset. And Olivia had said things too…

'Can I have my phone back just to send one text?' Suddenly it seemed desperately important that she contact her twin. 'Or could I use your computer? I haven't checked my emails for *two weeks.*'

'That isn't possible, Bella.'

'I'm going mad, Atif! Sand and silence are a lousy combination.' She glanced around her desperately and her attention focused on a cluster of low whitewashed buildings she'd noticed earlier in the week. 'How about those stables over there—can I at least go for a ride or something? Just for an hour.'

'They are nothing to do with the Retreat. The stables are privately owned.'

'Strange place to keep horses.' Bella studied the guards standing by the entrance. *Why would a stable need guards?* 'Well, if I can't borrow a horse could I at least have my iPod? I find it easier to relax to music.'

'Silence is golden.'

'Around here, everything is golden.' Simmering with frustration, Bella looked at the shifting sands and an idea took shape in her mind—*an outrageous, daring idea*. 'That city we passed through on the way here, tell me about it.'

'Al-Rafid is a sheikhdom, famous for its rich, cultural heritage.'

'Is there oil?' She forced herself to make casual conversation but all she really wanted to ask was, *How long will it take me to get there and do they have high-speed broadband?*

'Huge reserves of oil, but the ruling Sheikh is an astute businessman. He has turned what was once an ancient desert city into an international centre for commerce. The buildings on the waterfront are as modern as anything you would find in Manhattan or Canary Wharf, but only a few streets away is the old city with many wonderful examples of Persian architecture. Al-Rafid Palace is the most breathtaking of all, but it is rarely opened to the public because it is home to Sheikh Zafiq and his family.'

'Lucky him, living in a city. He obviously hates the sand too.'

'On the contrary, Sheikh Zafiq loves the desert, but he is a fiercely bright, educated man who has successfully incorporated progressive business thinking into the running of a very traditional country. But he has never forgotten his roots. For one week every year, he allows himself time alone in the desert. Time for reflection. He is a powerful man—some would say ruthless—but he is also a man deeply aware of his responsibilities.'

Responsibility…

Wasn't that the last word her father had said to her before he'd sent her into exile? Bella squirmed uncomfortably, trying to ease the sharp prick of her conscience. 'So…this sheikh. Is he married with eight wives and a hundred children?'

'His Highness has not yet chosen a wife. His family background is complicated.'

'I bet it's a picnic compared to mine.'

'Sheikh Zafiq's mother was a princess, much loved by everyone. Unfortunately she died when he was a baby.'

'She died?' Bella felt as though she'd been thumped in the chest. *Like her, he'd lost his mother as a child.* She felt compelled to find out more about the powerful, ruthless Sheikh, forgetting that her original objective had been simply to discover the distance to civilisation. 'Did his father marry again?'

'Yes, but tragically both his father and stepmother were killed in an accident when His Highness was just a teenager.'

So he'd lost *two* mothers.

Bella watched as the rising sun set fire to the dunes, changing the colours from dull red to bright gold. She felt a strange affinity with the mysterious Sheikh. He was out there somewhere across the bleak, featureless mountains of sand. Did he think about the mother he'd never known? Had *he* discovered things about her that would have been better left a secret?

Was his mind as much of a mess as hers?

Bella dug her hands into the pockets of her cotton trousers and reminded herself that regret was pointless. The past couldn't be undone. In all the hours of enforced meditation there was one topic on which she'd refused to allow herself to dwell.

Her mother.

Later. Later, she'd have to think about it but for now it was all too raw.

'So this Sheikh guy—' she pushed her hair out of her eyes, grimacing at the texture and indulging in a brief fantasy about deep conditioning and a blow dry '—he must have been pretty young to take over the running of a country.'

'Just eighteen. But he was bred to rule.'

'Poor guy. Must have had a pretty grim child-hood. But all that oil must mean he's rich. So why hasn't he married? I suppose he's old and ugly and can't even buy himself a wife.'

'His Highness is in his early thirties and is considered extremely handsome by those better qualified to comment on these things than me.'

'So what's wrong with him, then?' Bella eyed the lizard that scuttled across the sand in front of her.

'At some point he will marry someone suitable, but I understand that he is in no hurry.'

'And who can blame him? Marriage can be a nightmare. My father has done it three times. He's a devotee of the saying, "If at first you don't succeed—try, try and try again." You have to admire his perseverance. As a spectator sport it's quite gripping.'

'Your father has had three marriages?'

'You'd think he'd be good at it by now, wouldn't you?' Bella brushed sand from her bare arms, wondering whether it counted as exfoliation. 'He's had enough practise.'

'You have to let the anger go, Bella. You're too passionate.'

'That's me.' She kept her tone careless. 'Too passionate. Too…everything. Try having siblings, half-siblings, three mothers and a father like mine and you might understand why I don't have your sense of calm. Nothing winds you up like family. Except maybe having your laptop, your phone and your iPod removed at the same time.'

'It is when life is at its most demanding that we must seek inner peace. Your own ability for quiet reflection can be an oasis in the storm of life.'

'I wouldn't say no to a few days by an oasis,' Bella said absently, unsettled by the effect his words had on her. The truth was she envied his sense of calm. She wanted that, but had no idea how to achieve it. 'Palm trees, water to bathe in. I have no problem with sand, providing I'm staring down at it from my sun lounger with a Margarita in my hand.'

He bowed his head. 'I'll leave you to reflect, Bella. And see you at nine for yoga.'

'Yoga. Yippee. The excitement might just kill me.' Bella's expression was deadpan and she watched him stroll back towards the tents but inside she was boiling with emotion.

Enough!

No more meditation.

No more desert.

She was going to find the keys to a Jeep and

get out of here even if it meant tying someone up in their tent.

She was about to return to the Retreat and go on the hunt for transport when she noticed that the guards had disappeared from the entrance to the stables. Bella's eyes narrowed and her mind raced ahead as she adjusted her plans. No one knew her in the stables, did they? If she walked with enough confidence they might even think she worked there.

Indulging in a brief fantasy about fleeing across the desert in a horsebox, she slid past a sign that said "Strictly No Admittance" and walked down a sandy path that led to a stable block. A fountain bubbled in the centre of the deserted courtyard and only now could Bella see that the stables were both sophisticated and extensive.

'Whoever owns this place must be seriously loaded.' She sneaked a look over her shoulder to see if anyone had noticed her. But the stables appeared deserted. No guards. No one.

Strange, Bella thought, glancing around her. *Where was everyone?*

She knew from experience that stables were busy places.

A horse stuck its head over the door of the stable and whickered at her.

Bella walked across to him. 'At least someone lives here. Hello, beautiful,' she crooned, rubbing her hand over the mare's silky neck. 'How's your morning so far? Done any meditation? Knotted any of your legs into a lotus? Sipped any herbal tea?'

The horse blew gently against her neck and Bella suddenly felt better than she had for weeks.

'Want to come and sleep in my tent?' She kissed the animal on the nose, fussing and gentling the mare, the familiar scent of hay and horse calming her in a way that no amount of meditation had achieved. Peering over the stable door, she took in the quality of the horse. 'You really are a beauty. Pure-bred Arab. Why would anyone keep a horse as special as you hidden away out here?'

The horse nudged her hard and Bella almost lost her balance.

'You're fed up with being trapped in the stable, aren't you? I know the feeling. Where is every-one? Why are you on your own here?'

The place was eerily deserted and Bella looked around uneasily, trying to shake the feeling that something was very, very wrong—*that something bad was about to happen.*

'Oh, for crying out loud—' Cross with herself, she turned back to the horse. 'I've been living in boredomville for so long I'm imagining things. If there's one thing I've learned in the past two weeks it's that nothing ever happens out here.'

The horse moved restlessly in its box and Bella murmured to the animal sympathetically, sharing that restlessness. She had a desperate longing to spring onto her back and just ride and ride until her thoughts were far behind.

And why not? Why take a Jeep when she could *ride* to the city?

It couldn't be that far. She could remember the way. Vaguely. Once there she could arrange for the horse to be returned with her compliments.

Hopefully Atif would be so angry he'd refuse to have her back.

I'll be banned, Bella thought happily, sliding the bolt on the stable door and letting herself inside. Bad Bella. 'People always think the worst of me and I'd hate to disappoint them. Poor Atif is going to need to delve deep to discover his inner peace,' she told the mare as she swiftly untied her. 'I'm about to put his karma through significant turbulence. He'd better fasten his seat belt.'

'If you wish to spend a week alone in the desert, then at least allow your guards to accompany you, Zafiq.'

'If I allowed the guards to accompany me, then I would no longer be alone,' Zafiq pointed out drily. 'This is the one week of my life when I am allowed to be a man and not a ruler. I place you in sole charge, Rachid.'

His young brother paled, clearly daunted by the responsibility. 'You don't think you should postpone your trip? The oil negotiations have reached a crucial stage. They are expecting you to come back with a lower offer.'

'Then they will be disappointed.'

'You are seriously going to walk away at the peak of negotiations? It's the worst time.'

Zafiq gave a cool smile. 'On the contrary, it's the *best* time, Rachid.'

'What if they go elsewhere?'

'They won't.'

'But how can you be so sure? How do you know? How do you *always* know the right thing to do?' As they walked towards the stables, his brother cast him an envious glance. 'I wish I could be as inscrutable as you. You *never* reveal your emotions.'

Hearing the angry squeal of a stallion, Zafiq walked purposefully in the direction of the commotion. 'The same cannot be said for my horse,

who seems to be revealing his emotions unhin-
dered.'

'Everyone in the stables is terrified of him.'

Zafiq watched as his Master of Horse led the
half-wild, prancing stallion into the yard. Noticing
the stallion's ears flatten angrily, he sighed. 'It
seems Batal needs a break as much as I do.'
Without hesitating he strode towards the horse,
his brother following at a safe distance.

'Do you ever worry about anything?' Rachid
blurted the words out as if he'd been bottling
them up for days. 'Was there ever a time when
you felt like me?'

Zafiq reflected on that question, a grim smile
touching his mouth. He could have told his brother
that his childhood had felt like nothing more than
a rigorous training camp for instilling a sense of
responsibility and duty.

'Confidence comes with experience. I have had
plenty of experience.' With that economical response, he watched as Batal pawed the ground,
nostrils flared. 'Release him.' As the sweating
stable staff sprang out of the way, he put his hand
on the animal's neck and the stallion shuddered
and calmed.

'Horses and women—' Rachid grinned at him
in admiration. 'How do you do it?'

Zafiq ignored the question, vaulting onto the animal's back with athletic ease. 'I will be back in five days. And Rachid—' his hand closed around the reins as he stilled the restless stallion '—this is your opportunity to gain experience of your own. Don't waste it. And try not to start a war.'

Without giving his brother time to voice any more objections, Zafiq allowed the shivering, expectant horse to spring forward, not bothering to rein him in as he plunged forwards through the open gates that led straight from the palace into the desert. The animal gave two ferocious bucks, but Zafiq didn't shift in the saddle and the stallion settled down, as if remembering that he'd met his match in this particular rider.

'You're as impatient as I am to leave the city,' Zafiq murmured, enjoying the surge of adrenalin that came with the sudden burst of speed.

The desert opened up before him, the space offering sanctuary from the oppressive demands of state business and the pressures of caring for his young brothers and sisters, whose needs appeared to become more complicated as they grew up, rather than less. As their guardian, he felt a burden of responsibility towards them that was in every way equal to the one he felt for his country.

After eleven punishing months of responsibility and duty, he was ready to leave it all behind and indulge in the yearly solitude he richly deserved and rarely enjoyed.

No problems. No pressure.

Just the desert and his own company.

Lost.

Heat, thirst, sand, heat, thirst, sand…

Shouldn't she be there by now? She'd been riding for hours and it all looked the same.

Whatever had possessed her to think she'd be able to find her way?

Her mouth was drier than the desert, her head throbbed and her eyes stung.

Bella squinted dizzily into the blazing sun, focusing on the shimmer of heat that seemed to make the landscape move. What she really needed now was an oasis with cool water and palm trees offering a generous cocoon of shade. But there was nothing except sand, heat and the desperate burning thirst that grew more acute by the minute.

Her mouth was so dry she would even have welcomed herbal tea.

She'd stopped guiding the horse and was only

dimly aware that the animal was still walking purposefully.

'I'm sorry,' she moaned, leaning forward and burying her burning face in the mare's mane. 'I don't care about me but I'm really sorry I've done this to you. Why aren't you fitted with sat nav? Stop walking. There's no point. We might as well just give up.'

The horse gave a snort of disapproval and continued to walk. Bella was too weak and exhausted to do anything about it.

She was going to die.

Her body was going to be buried under the sand and discovered centuries later by archaeologists digging for relics.

Despite her dizzy, dehydrated state the inevitable headlines flashed into her head: *Bad Bella Balfour Disappears from Desert Retreat.*

Perhaps they'd think she'd drowned herself in herbal tea.

Perhaps they wouldn't even care.

She gave a weak moan and tried to say something to the horse but by now her mouth was so dry it was difficult to speak. The pain in her head was so severe she felt as though someone was attacking her with an axe and her vision blurred.

The last thing she saw before she slid from the

horse was an ominous black shadow emerging through the golden haze.

Death, she thought dizzily, and landed on the sand unconscious.

CHAPTER TWO

ZAFIQ sprang from his horse and issued a low command. The stallion immediately threw up his head proudly and stood still, his tail held high.

Taking in the identity of the other horse, Zafiq's initial shock turned to raw, undiluted fury. 'Amira—' His voice gentle, he approached his favourite mare, hand outstretched, his anger ruthlessly contained. 'What are you doing all the way out here?' The horse allowed him to take the reins and he swiftly tied the animal to the saddle of his own mount.

Later, he promised himself with icy focus. *Later, there would be a price to pay for this.* For now, his priority had to be the girl.

She was the most unlikely looking horse thief he'd ever seen.

One glance at her thin cotton clothing was sufficient to tell him that she knew nothing about surviving in the harsh, unforgiving desert, and his mouth tightened as he bent over her inert body.

A pink baseball cap lay in the sand some

distance from where she'd fallen but apart from that one small concession to the heat of the sun she appeared to have nothing in the way of protection.

Zafiq's lip curled in contempt. After all the threats and warnings, *this* was who'd they sent to kidnap his most valued horse?

Impatience mingling with anger he glanced around for a rucksack, or something that indicated the girl had packed liquid, but there was nothing.

Muttering under his breath he stooped and lifted her, the breath hissing through his teeth as her blonde hair trailed over his arm like a shaft of light from a single sunbeam. Sand dusted her flushed cheeks and his eyes rested on her dry lips.

Unable to look away from the generous curve of her mouth, Zafiq felt a dangerous heat explode inside him and he stared down at her beautiful face, momentarily forgetting everything except the woman in his arms. And then her eyelids flickered upwards and he found himself staring into the bluest eyes he'd ever seen. They were eyes that reminded him of a summer sky, of the azure blue of the Arabian Sea, of the cerulean silk that was sold in the souks of Al-Rafid. But despite the intense colour those eyes were dull, dazed and her lips parted and she whispered something—nothing that made sense; something about herbal tea—and then her eyes closed and she didn't say another word.

Aware that he was still staring down at her face, Zafiq felt a rush of anger.

What sort of a man was he?

The girl was unconscious.

She was half dead, and he was thirsting for her as she was no doubt thirsting for water.

Dehydration, he thought savagely, holding her easily as he walked back to his stallion and removed a bottle from his saddlebag. He'd seen it before, too many times.

'Drink,' he ordered harshly, but she gave no sign that she was able to obey his command.

Questioning what crime he'd committed to be saddled with an unconscious girl at a time when he was supposed to be enjoying solitude, Zafiq splashed a small amount of water over her lips and watched with grim satisfaction as her tongue flickered out. At least he wasn't dealing with a corpse.

He wanted her to live so that she could face justice for trying to steal his horse. She *would* pay the price for her crime.

In order to keep her alive, he needed to get her out of the sun and cool her down. And the only place he could do that was in his own camp.

Resigning himself to the inevitable, Zafiq swung her limp body onto his horse and supported her while he vaulted on behind her. Drawing her lifeless body against the power of his own, he closed his legs on the stallion's flanks and urged him forwards, glancing over his shoulder to check on the mare.

It took less than twenty minutes to reach the shelter of his remote desert camp—twenty minutes during which he discovered to his frustration that he was able to become aroused by an unconscious woman.

Dismounting in a fluid movement, Zafiq gritted his teeth as he lifted her once again into his arms.

Perhaps he should have left her in the desert.

Turning the horses loose to find shade and water in the small oasis, he carried the unconscious girl towards his tent, breathing through his mouth in order to block out the tantalising floral scent of her hair. He dumped her gently on the mat that served as a bed and frowned impatiently as she lay still, not moving.

Torn between concern and exasperation, Zafiq

leant forward and placed his fingers on her forehead. Registering the dry, burning heat, he realised that if he didn't cool her down, he was going to have a serious problem on his hands.

'I don't know who you are, but you clearly have more beauty than sense,' he growled, striding across the tent to fetch a bowl of tepid water and a piece of cloth.

So much for a week of peace, solitude and quiet reflection.

Zafiq dipped the cloth in the water and bathed her face and neck. Knowing that her recovery was dependent on cooling and rehydration, he reluctantly unfastened the buttons of her long sleeve shirt. Peeling it away he bathed her slender arms, keeping his eyes averted from the pretty lace bra that was now the only barrier between him and her body. He left her arms and body damp, allowing the water droplets to cool her overheated skin.

At this rate he was going to need the cool water himself, he thought, *seriously* unsettled by the effect she had on him. With haste and clinical efficiency he tugged her white cotton trousers past the curve of her hips and down her long legs.

'Atif?' She murmured a man's name and Zafiq

frowned sharply, wondering whether there had been someone else out in the desert with her.

Of course. She must have had an accomplice. A plan to kidnap his horse couldn't have been executed by one lone woman, could it?

Wondering what had happened to his usual clarity of thought, Zafiq dropped the cloth back into the bowl and raked her flushed cheeks with an impatient gaze, but this time his impatience was directed towards himself. Since when had he ceased to think logically?

Driven by concern and the pressing need to extract information, he scooped her up and pressed the cup of water to her lips. 'Drink,' he ordered, and although her eyes remained closed she obediently parted her lips and swallowed. 'And more.' He continued to encourage her to drink and then laid her gently back against the pillows and bathed her once again.

Shaded by the tent and cooled by the water she started to revive.

Only when he judged that she was able to answer, did Zafiq scoop her up once again and voice the question that was troubling him.

'Who was with you?' His voice was rough—rougher than he intended—but even so she didn't respond. Trying to ignore the softness of her skin against his arms, Zafiq tried again. 'Were you alone?'

Her eyes slid to his and she looked at him with those stunning blue eyes that were undeniably designed to drive a man to distraction.

'Horse—' she croaked, and Zafiq felt the tension ripple across his shoulders.

'I know about the horse. What about humans?'

Her tongue moistened her lower lip, slowly, as if speaking were the hardest thing she'd ever done. 'Is the horse OK?'

She was lying half dead in his arms and yet she was asking about the horse?

Momentarily thrown by that surprising fact, it took Zafiq a moment to realise that she obviously had a vested interest in the animal's welfare. 'She is fine, although no thanks to you. You will not be profiting on this occasion.'

'Profiting?'

'There are many questions which you will answer in time, but first tell me about Atif. Who is he?'

Her eyes closed again but not before he'd seen tears glistening and the dull sheen of despair.

'Please don't make me go back.'

'Go back where?' Accustomed to receiving an immediate answer to any question he posed,

Zafiq found this laborious process of dragging information from her unspeakably tedious.

What sort of man would leave it to a woman to steal a horse?

Or had she seduced someone to achieve her objective?

Irritated by his thoughts, he pressed the cup to her lips again. Her hand closed over his wrist as she drank and the burn of her fingers against his skin induced a reaction so shockingly powerful that Zafiq almost dropped the cup.

'How could you have done this without help? There must have been someone with you?'

'No.' Her voice was faint. 'On my own.'

As he laid her back against the pillows, Zafiq pondered why a horse thief should be working alone and unsupported. All the intelligence he'd received on the threat to his valuable mare had seemed to point to a group of people. 'Sleep.' He rose to his feet swiftly, needing to distance himself. *Needing to regain control.* 'I must check on the animals.'

No one would be touching his horses again, he promised himself fiercely as he strode towards the entrance of the tent.

'Wait—' Her soft croak stopped him. 'Who are you?'

Zafiq gave a cynical smile.

Never before had anyone asked him that question. He eyed her blonde hair and fair skin thoughtfully. It was entirely possible that this uninformed, naive woman, who thought she could kidnap a valuable animal without detection, genuinely had no idea who he was.

Which suited him.

His exact location was a secret. And he wanted it to remain a secret, particularly as he now had Amira's safety to think about.

'I'm your nemesis,' he purred, his voice lethally soft as he lifted the flap of the tent. 'And you are going to live to regret the day you stole my horse.'

Everything had shifted from gold to white.

Had she died and gone to heaven?

Bella blinked several times and realised that she was staring up at canvas. She was inside a tent. And it was hot. Stiflingly hot, like being trapped in an oven on full heat with the door closed. Her head throbbed, her mouth felt parched and she had no idea what she was doing here. Memories flickered through her head—a strong male voice ordering her to drink, firm, decisive hands stripping her of her clothing…

Stripping her of her clothing?

Realising that she was naked apart from her underwear, she was about to find something to cover herself with when the flap of the tent was pushed aside and a man strode inside. Stripped to the waist, his muscular bronzed shoulders glistened with water, as though wet from a dip in the pool. He was naked apart from a towel tied loosely around his lean hips.

For a moment she thought she must be hallucinating because he was indecently, *impossibly*, handsome.

'OK, maybe I *have* died and gone to heaven,' Bella croaked humorously but there was no answering smile from her rescuer. Eyes as dark as jet scanned her with arrogant appraisal and unconcealed disdain.

'You have a strange concept of heaven. Or maybe you don't realise how much trouble you're in.'

'You are my kind of trouble—' Feeling weak and dizzy, Bella eyed his powerful physique and started to laugh. 'You have to see the funny side—all those hours I've spent at parties hoping to meet a spectacular-looking man and he turns up here in the desert—' The desert.

Oh, God, she was still in the desert.

Catching the flare of shock in his eyes, she sighed as everything rushed back to her. 'Look, I've no idea where I am, but just tell me you're not going to make me drink herbal tea and search for the meaning of life. Otherwise I'll have a relapse.' Conscious of the contrast between his striking good looks and her dishevelled appearance, Bella surreptitiously slid her fingers through her hair, wincing as she encountered a dry, matted mass. 'Ugh. Sand. There's sand everywhere.'

'That's why it's called the desert.'

'Yes, but it's even in my *hair*—' Her trademark silky mane had the texture of sandpaper and Bella shuddered.

No wonder he wasn't looking at her the way men usually looked at her.

'A few hours ago you were staring death in the face and now you are worrying about your hair?' The contempt in his tone added insult to injury.

'Look, do you have any idea what it's like to be stranded in this red, gritty wilderness without so much as a bottle of decent conditioner?' Bella pouted at him and then lifted her fingers to her mouth in horror. 'My lips are cracked—'

'That's what happens when you trek across the desert without appropriate protection.' He was as harsh and blistering as the desert sun and Bella's spine stiffened defensively.

'I hadn't planned on getting lost!'

'That tends to happen when you point your horse in the wrong direction.' His sardonic tone was the final straw and Bella felt her cheeks redden.

'Your bedside manner needs work.'

'The quality of my bedside manner,' he drawled, 'depends on who is lying in my bed.'

A stranger to masculine indifference, Bella was appalled to feel a lump settle in her throat. She reminded herself frantically that red tear-stained eyes in a sandblasted face would make her look like a gargoyle and swallowed hard, refusing to give in to an emotion that would make her even less physically appealing.

Give me half an hour in that pool he's just swum in, she thought to herself, *and I'll knock him dead.* Even without the aid of a mirror.

'Are you always this preoccupied with your appearance? One would have thought you had more important issues on your mind. Like humility. You should be dwelling on the lesson the desert has taught you.' The slow-burning anger in his eyes made her wonder what she'd done to offend him so deeply.

'The desert has taught me never to leave the

city again.' Feeling sicker by the minute, Bella stretched gingerly and discovered that she ached from head to toe. 'You don't seem very pleased that I'm alive.'

'I was not expecting to spend my first night in the desert with a half-dead female.'

'You prefer completely dead females? I suppose at least they don't answer back.' Sneaking a look at his unsmiling face, Bella decided there was no point in asking if he had a mirror. 'Look, I'm sorry I've messed up your plans, OK? Just give me something for my headache, point me towards the city and I'll get out of your way.'

He muttered something in a language she didn't understand and this time his glance was both fierce and contemptuous. 'Have you learned nothing from your escapade? This is the desert, not the English countryside. You don't just go for a walk. Or even a ride.'

Bella remembered the dark shadow emerging from the haze of sunlight and realised that it must have been him. '*You* do.'

'I was born in this country. I understand every movement of the sun and every shift of the sands and yet even I would not set out on a journey as lamentably ill equipped as you. Next time you decide to commit a crime I suggest you spend more time on the planning. You had no map, no spare clothing and no water.' Incredulity and disgust radiated from his expression and his tone. *'What were you thinking?'*

'I suppose I wasn't really thinking,' Bella admitted, chastened by his harsh words and distracted by the word *crime*. 'I just wanted to get to the city. I misunderstood the distance.'

'And that one small error would have cost two lives if I hadn't arrived when I did.'

'Two?' As she absorbed the meaning behind his statement, Bella struggled to a sitting position, guilt sharpening her anxiety. 'Wait a minute. The beautiful horse—is she all right? You said—'

'She will survive, but no thanks to you. That mare is a valuable animal.' His smile was cynical. 'But you know that, don't you? That's why you took her.'

'I took her because she was so friendly.' Bella was tortured by the horror of what might have happened. She'd almost killed a horse. She'd totally and utterly messed up. Again. But no one would be surprised to hear that, would they? Everyone expected her to mess up. 'She's full Arab isn't she? They have such distinctive features.'

'And I'm sure you were well acquainted with

her distinctive features. How else would you be sure of stealing the right animal?'

'You're right to be angry with me.' Bella was genuinely contrite and more than a little puzzled by the venom in his tone. 'I'm angry with myself. I would never intentionally have put the mare in danger. I love horses—much more than humans actually,' she said humbly, 'but I honestly thought it would take me less than an hour to get to the city.'

'Was that where they were waiting?'

'Who?'

'Your accomplices.'

'I didn't have any accomplices.'

'Then how did you plan to sell her?'

'I wasn't going to sell her!' Bella sat up straight, offended by the suggestion. 'I was going to send her back to the stables.'

Exasperation mingled with incredulity. 'You expect me to believe that you stole a horse with the intention of returning her?'

'I didn't steal a horse!' Bella's voice was an outraged squeak. 'I—I just borrowed her. For a short time...' Her voice trailed off, her pathetic defence squashed by the satanic blaze of his beautiful black eyes. 'I'm *not* a thief!'

'You were in possession of an animal that does

not belong to you. Had she escaped from her stable?'

Bella shrank slightly. 'Er, no.'

'So you physically took her?'

'I *borrowed* her—' Seriously worried now, Bella wished she had a weapon so that she could defend herself. And then she remembered he was a man. And she had big blue eyes. What better weapon could a girl ask for? She angled her face and looked directly at him. 'I can explain…'

One eyebrow raised, he folded his arms. 'Rarely have I been so intrigued to hear an excuse.'

Perhaps he hadn't looked at her properly. Bella widened her eyes slightly but his hard gaze didn't flicker.

She must be too far away from him. Still, there was always her hair. Her long, blonde hair. Bella tried to flick her hair over her shoulder but it was so stiff with sand it barely moved.

Realising that she was going to have to rely on her wits, not her looks, she felt her insides quail. 'I was stuck in this place in the middle of nowhere—'

'What was it called?'

'The Retreat.' Bella shuddered. 'It's an alternative, yoga…thingy—a drive-you-mad place—'

'It is a world-renowned centre for contemplative meditation.'

'That too.' Bella discreetly removed some sand from inside her nails and grimaced with distaste. 'Anyway, there was sand everywhere—sand, sand and more sand.'

'In the time it is taking you to voice your excuse, the entire landscape of the desert will have altered,' he drawled, and Bella glared at him.

'You're *so* unsympathetic. I suppose you're going to tell me you love the sand.'

'I have too little time to enjoy it.'

'How much time is too little? A nanosecond? I don't think I ever want to see a grain of sand again. And that's why I borrowed the horse. I just had to get out of there! I doubt I'll ever be able to look at a beach again. I'll be taking city breaks from now on.'

His gaze hardened. 'So you just walked into a busy stable and helped yourself to a horse.'

'Actually, that was really weird.' Bella wrinkled her nose as she remembered how odd it had seemed to her at the time. 'The place was deserted. A bit spooky actually. No one around. It was as if something was about to happen—' she gave a shrug '—but that was probably wishful thinking. Nothing ever happened in that place,

I can tell you. My imagination must have been playing tricks.'

'It's heartening to know that you are capable of imagination—' But he seemed distracted, as if something she'd said had captured his attention. 'So you are saying that no one was there? That you simply walked into the yard, took the horse and rode into the desert?'

'Yes. Whoever is running that stable should fire some of the staff because they were really lax. I mean, what if one of the horses was sick or something?'

'Indeed.'

'Anyway, so I rode into the desert, following the track to the city. Except it obviously wasn't the right track. It all looks the same. And then I realised I was lost. If you hadn't come along when you did—'

'You would be dead.' His blunt appraisal made her shiver.

'Yes. Very probably. So, thanks again. I'm lucky you found me.'

He watched her for a long moment, as though he were making his mind up about something, and then he strode across the tent, pulled open a canvas bag and removed a robe. Intercepting her stare, his mouth tightened. 'You might want to look away.'

'Why would I want to do that?' Bella's wicked side took over, driving her into territory she knew she would have been better avoiding. 'You have a fantastic body.'

Shock flared in his eyes and dark streaks of colour highlighted his magnificent cheekbones. 'And you play a dangerous game for a woman alone and unprotected. Perhaps I am not a good man to be trapped with, *habibiti*.' His voice was suddenly soft and there was a shimmer of mockery in his jet-black eyes. He slid the robe over his head in a fluid movement, somehow managing to discard the towel at the same time. 'I believe you have a saying: "out of the frying pan into the fire."'

Bella's mouth dried as she watched him slide a dagger into the folds of his robe and her stomach fluttered with nerves. 'Well, it's certainly true that in the past few hours I've been fried, sautéed and flambéed.' Her weak attempt at humour again fell flat and she flopped back against the pillows, her head throbbing and her bravado wearing thin. 'All right, I get the message. No humour allowed. But you ought to know it's polite to at least smile when someone makes a joke.' She wanted to ask why he needed a dagger, but she wasn't sure she wanted to hear the answer.

He was a complete contrast to the men she usually met—a lethal combination of untamed man and raw sexuality. *A real man*, she thought to herself, distracted by the dark shadow that emphasised the strong lines of his jaw. It was hard to imagine him sitting at a desk in a tall city office, but she had no problem imagining him wrestling a wild animal with his bare hands. Embarrassed to admit that she found him astonishingly attractive, Bella put her hands over her eyes and gave a groan. She was the ultimate modern city girl and here she was lusting over macho man.

The heat must have finally got to her.

'I'm surprised you find your situation amusing.' His gaze held hers. 'You're lost and you have absolutely no idea where you are.'

'I'm not lost. I'm with you.'

'And that gives you no cause for alarm?' His cool voice held a dangerous edge. 'I could be a greater threat to your safety than being lost in the desert. There is no one else near you. No one to rescue you. No one to hear you scream.'

Bella burst out laughing. 'You sound as though you're doing a voice-over for a horror movie.'

'I am merely pointing out that a healthy dose of caution might increase your life expectancy.'

'I've lived in London and New York. I'm street-wise.'

His smile was slow and deadly. 'You are not in London or New York now. You are in the middle of the Arabian Desert with a man you don't know. And outside this tent there are poisonous snakes, scorpions and enough sand to swallow you whole and never again reveal your body.'

His words made her shiver and Bella rubbed her hands over her arms, growing more alarmed by the minute. 'Stop trying to scare me. Do you want a hysterical woman in your tent?'

'I don't want a woman in my tent at all.'

'Oh—' Bella relaxed slightly. 'I get it. You're gay.'

Incredulity flared in his dark eyes. 'I am *not* gay. But nor did I seek company on this trip. I value solitude.'

'Really?' For a moment she was fascinated. 'You mean you actually *want* to be on your own?'

'Time for reflection is a gift.'

Bella pulled a face. 'In my opinion, reflection is an overrated pastime. I prefer being around people.'

'So what were you doing in the Retreat?'

'I was sent there.'

'By…?'

'Look, do we have to talk about this? The place was bad enough when I was there, without having to think about it afterwards. My brain is tired of examining itself. I'm allergic to meditation. Life is difficult enough without reflecting on it.' Bella watched as he poured himself a glass of water. Every movement he made was assured and con-fident, and although he was quite staggeringly good-looking, he was far too serious for her.

And now he was looking at her with the same expression of grim disapproval that her father used whenever she saw him.

Bella closed her eyes, the throb in her head worsening by the minute.

She heard him step towards her. 'How bad is that headache?'

'Headache? What headache? I don't have a headache.' She would rather have died than admit weakness to this stony-faced, austere sex god. 'I've never felt better in my life.'

'You're dehydrated. Drink more water.'

Bella contemplated ignoring his advice but the pain tearing through her head was growing worse so she reached for the cup that he'd placed on the floor by the bed. 'How come you have so much water with you?'

'I came prepared. Unlike you. I'm not accustomed to having to repeat a question—who sent you to the Retreat?'

'My father sent me.' She took another sip of water, tempted to ask him how much water it would take to cure the headache. 'I was supposed to find myself.'

'Instead of which you lost yourself.' His sardonic smile turned his face from handsome to breathtaking and Bella found it impossible to look away. He really was stunning. In fact, she had an uneasy feeling that his eyes might be even more beautiful than hers. If she didn't have a vile headache and he wasn't so moody, she'd definitely be interested.

Slightly unsettled by that realisation, she put the cup down carefully, trying not to spill any of the precious liquid. 'Thank you for rescuing me.'

'I had no choice. You collapsed in my path.'

He stood watching her from the end of the bed and it was impossible to miss the air of command that clung to him. 'So who are you?'

Bella's eyes widened again, but this time in amazement. No one had ever had to ask who she was before. *Everyone* knew who she was. Everywhere she went she was followed, photographed and criticised. People who had never even met her thought they knew her. Everyone had an opinion of her—almost always bad.

But out here in the wild sands of the desert, her face meant nothing.

It occurred to Bella that, at this precise moment, no one knew where she was. No one was watching her. No one was waiting for the scandalous Balfour twin to slip up. The headline writers of the newspapers were probably sitting bored at their desks, wondering who to write about.

An unusual sense of freedom settled over her.

Feeling liberated, she gave a wide smile. 'I'm Kate,' she said impulsively. 'And you are…?'

'And who is Olivia? And what is it you don't want her to do?'

Reminded of the situation that had brought her to the desert, Bella's euphoria dimmed. 'How do you know about Olivia?'

'While you were delirious with the heat, you talked. You kept saying, "No, Olivia, don't do it. Don't do it." Who is Olivia?'

'Just someone I know,' Bella whispered, her body trembling. Suddenly she wondered just how much she'd revealed. 'What else did I say?' Had she talked about her other sister Zoe? Had she said anything else about that terrible night?

'Nothing much. Did no one know you were leaving the Retreat?'

'No.' Bella thought back to the conversation she'd had with Atif. 'But I think they'll guess.'

'And they will send out a search party,' her rescuer snapped, 'which is the last thing we want.'

'I agree! If they find me they'll just drag me back for more torture—' Her eyes narrowed speculatively as she thought about what he'd just said. 'Wait a minute. Why wouldn't you want a search party to find me? It shouldn't bother you, unless…you don't want anyone to know where you are…' Her mind working, she rubbed her fingers along her forehead, trying to ease the pain in her head. 'And if you don't want anyone to know where you are, it means that normally people *do* know where you are, which in turn means that you're either a dangerous murderer on the run from justice, or you're someone important—'

'I haven't yet been driven to murder anyone,' he gritted, 'but that moment could be fast approaching. You clearly do have a very agile imagination and you talk a great deal for someone who was almost unconscious a few moments ago.'

'I have remarkable powers of recovery. So if you're not a criminal, then you must be famous.' Bella drew her legs up and rested her chin on her arms, determined not to reveal just how ill she was feeling. 'You're the Sheikh, aren't you? That's why you don't want anyone to know where you are.' Watching closely, she saw his immediate withdrawal. His shoulders straightened and his eyes were suddenly blank.

'What do you know about the Sheikh?'

'Very little. But Atif told me you spend a week every year in the desert.' She gave a soft gasp of understanding. 'That's why you don't want a search party, isn't it? This is your week in the desert and you don't want anyone to know where you are.'

'You are making a great number of assumptions.'

'All of which are right. There's no need to get defensive. I know all about wanting to avoid people. And I know how to keep secrets.' Bella rubbed her fingers over her cheeks and grimaced as she felt how dry her skin was. 'I'll do you a deal. I won't say I saw you, if you don't say you saw me.'

'This is *not* a joke.'

'Neither is my headache.' Exhausted from the

conversation, Bella flopped back onto the bed and closed her eyes. 'Stop glaring at me. You're very bad tempered. That's what meditation does for you. You should try thinking less.'

'Perhaps you should try thinking *more*, and then you would not find yourself in such scrapes.'

Deciding that it was time to get herself out of this mess, Bella swung her legs out of bed, stood and promptly collapsed in an undignified heap on the floor of the tent. 'Oops. Horizontal again and I haven't even had a drink.' She kept up the banter, too proud to admit how ill she felt. 'Look, just point me towards Al—whatever it's called, and I'll be out of your way. You can go back to your life and I can go back to mine.' Although what she was going to do with no source of income, she had no idea. Her father had cut off her allowance.

If she was at home she would have called one of the glossy magazines and offered herself for a cover shoot, but that wasn't exactly an option in the desert.

Did anyone employ models in this part of the world?

Even if they did, they weren't going to find her attractive at the moment.

He obviously didn't.

Strong hands lifted her to her feet. 'Given that you don't have the strength to cross the tent, how do you propose to make this journey safely?'

'Just lend me a horse. I'll be fine.' Overcome by a wave of dizziness, Bella looked for something to lean on. The only solid object seemed to be his chest, so she used that. Feeling hard muscle and solid male strength, awareness sliced through her, taking her by surprise. 'You smell *really* good,' she muttered. 'But I guess women tell you that all the time.'

He said something in a language she didn't understand and the next minute he'd released her and she crumpled to the floor in a heap again.

'All right, maybe women don't tell you that all the time.'

He'd pushed her away. *Men never pushed her away.*

It was always the other way round.

Still battling with the terrible dizziness, she risked a glance at him and clashed with furious black eyes.

'You have no idea how to behave.'

'You're right.' Bella dug her nails into her legs, fighting back a sudden rush of nausea. Oh, God, she felt hideously ill. And she was stuck with a man with a bad attitude and a dagger. 'You'd better get rid of me. Just lend me a horse and I'm out of here.'

'I will *not* lend you a horse.'

'Why not?' Her pride severely dented by his rejection, Bella suddenly wished she had access to her bathroom at Balfour Manor. And her hairdresser. Then this arrogant man wouldn't have been in such a hurry to push her away. Deciding that extra charm was needed to compensate for her sunburned face and sandy hair, she treated him to her most seductive smile. 'You don't need *two* horses. That's just greedy.'

'My stallion would kill you in minutes, and the mare is too valuable to risk with a novice.'

Affronted by his derogatory tone, Bella was about to confess that she knew a great deal about horses but decided that the less he knew about her the better.

She was feeling sicker and dizzier by the minute and it was dawning on her that she was stranded in the desert at the mercy of this stranger who thought she was a horse thief. 'I just want to get back to the city. I could make it in a couple of hours.'

'It takes longer than a couple of hours.' His tone dripped acid and he paced to the far side of the tent, every line of his powerful frame rigid with tension as he contemplated the situation. 'Without an escort, you would not make it.'

Bella struggled to stand, wavering like a new-born foal yet to become acquainted with its legs. Ignoring the obvious challenges of playing the seductress when it was difficult to put one leg in front of the other, she walked across to him. 'Then won't you escort me? Please?' Her voice coaxing, she placed her hand on his biceps and felt hard, solid muscle under her fingers.

He was strong. *Really strong.*

Without thinking what she was doing, she slid her fingertips slowly over his arm, fascinated by his physical strength.

The breath hissed through his teeth and he looked down at her, the raw sexuality in his shimmering gaze punching the breath from her body.

Chemistry arced between them and Bella responded to his unmistakably male appraisal with a slow, feminine smile.

So he *wasn't* immune.

It was a boost to her confidence to know that even without the help of her hairdresser, she could still twist a man around her little finger.

You're going to be giving me that horse as a

gift in a minute, she thought with a flash of relief, peeping at him from under her lashes.

It was a look that had never failed her. Even without the extra help of mascara, she was optimistic that she could work her usual magic.

'I know you'll help me,' she said breathlessly, deciding that a man as macho as him would respond best to a weak-female-in-trouble approach. All she needed to do was take advantage of his need to feel like a man and at least flirting took her mind off the fact she was lost in the desert with a stranger.

Searching for just the right phrase to boost a fragile ego, she gave a faltering smile. 'I—I don't think I can cope by myself.'

He didn't return the smile. 'Given that I've already had to rescue you once, I don't need you to tell me that you can't cope by yourself. I have reached that conclusion without assistance.'

Angry, Bella turned red. And now she was trapped. If she snapped that she was *perfectly* capable of looking after herself, then there was no way he'd help her.

Frustrated, she decided that the only other trick worth trying was agreeing with him. Men liked that, didn't they? It made them feel clever.

Ignoring her inner woman who was gearing up

to slap his arrogant face, she lifted her blue eyes
to his, switching her expression to helpless.

'You're right.' She conjured up her most pathetic
voice. 'I can't cope. I'm a disaster.' Trying not to
reflect on the fact that her father would actually
have agreed with that statement, Bella cleared
her throat and added extra weight to her image
of vulnerability by fluttering her eyelashes.

'You seem to be having some sort of problem
with your eyes,' he drawled. 'Is it sand? If so, then
I recommend that you splash them with water.'

Bella couldn't help it. She burst out laughing.
'So you *do* have a sense of humour under that
severe exterior.'

'I'm not laughing.'

'Well, you should! It would do you good! You're
way too grumpy. Oh, just forget it. Flirting with
you is too much like hard work,' Bella said crossly,
seriously worried that she seemed to have lost the
only skill she possessed. 'If you won't help me,
I'll just go by myself!'

'An interesting transformation. Innocent to independent in one blink of an eyelash. You're a
very manipulative woman. And slow to learn.'

Bella gasped. 'I'm *not* slow!'

'But you admit to being manipulative. Interesting.' His smile lacked humour. 'The only way

you will make it out of this desert alive is if you are escorted.'

'Then escort me,' she said sweetly, peeping at him from under her lashes, but his answering gaze was hard and unyielding.

'Is that what men do when you look at them? Do they roll over and say yes?'

'The rolling over part usually comes after the yes,' Bella said flippantly, feeling her anxiety increase by the minute. *He just didn't respond to her the way other men did.*

'Your morals are clearly as suspect as your judgement.'

'There's nothing wrong with my judgement.'

'You chose to ride through a desert. That behaviour borders on the insane.' He extracted himself from her grip with a deliberate movement and Bella looked at him in dismay, horrified to discover that the lump was back in her throat.

Her life had fallen apart and she appeared to have lost the only thing she'd ever been sure of. Her ability to attract men. And that was all she had, wasn't it? That was her gift. She wasn't clever like her sister Annie; she wasn't sweet and kind like Emily, or practical like Olivia....

She had blue eyes. She had blonde hair. And the combination had stopped working. Feeling incredibly vulnerable, she looked away. 'Look, you obviously hate me and that's fine. I don't care. Surely that's all the more reason to escort me back to the city where you'll never have to see me again. I promise I won't be any trouble—'

And finally he laughed. 'The word could have been invented just for you. You have *trouble* written all over you.'

'Then the sooner you escort me out of your life, the better,' Bella said hopefully and he shook his head, still laughing.

'You just can't help it, can you? You have to flirt. I'm tempted to give you seven veils just to see how far you're prepared to go to get what you want.'

Distracted by how *seriously* attractive he was when he laughed, Bella stared at him. 'Do women really dance for you? Using veils?'

'People do whatever I want them to do,' he said silkily, and she felt her stomach perform a series of elaborate acrobatics.

'More fool them. I wouldn't dance for you.'

His smile was supremely confident. 'I'm the ruling sheikh. If I order you to dance, you'll dance.'

'And if I refuse?' *It was weird*, she mused,

this combination of raw fear and shocking chemistry.

His smile faded and he looked at her with disturbing intensity. 'You are wilful and reckless.'

'Absolutely right.' Abandoning the helpless woman act, Bella tried a different approach. 'You don't want me around. As you say, I'm more trouble than I'm worth. So why don't you just lend me the friendly horse that isn't likely to kill me and I'll go and be wilful and reckless somewhere you can't see me.'

They stared at each other for a long, tense moment.

Then he surprised her by taking her face in his hands.

His fingers were firm and strong on her face and Bella wondered if he could feel the frantic beat of her heart. Did she have a pulse anywhere near his fingers?

A slow, heavy weakness spread through her limbs but she knew that the lethargy had nothing to do with her recent spell in the desert and the feeling shocked her because she never felt anything for men. She used them, the way they used her.

His gaze held hers. 'I'll escort you back to the city—'

Hypnotised by his velvety dark eyes, Bella felt a rush of relief. 'Thank you so much, you're a really wonderful person. I knew it the moment you walked into the tent. I knew that all that scary warrior stuff was all an act. And that dagger is obviously ornamental. I bet it isn't even sharp—'

'Do you always interrupt people?'

'Often,' Bella breathed, distracted by the beauty of his eyes. 'Sorry, what were we saying? Oh, yes…interrupting—it's one of my many faults. But I'm working on it.'

'Then you might like to work a little harder.' His thumb traced a circle over her cheek. 'I said that I'll escort you back to the city—'

'I heard you. And I—' Bella felt his fingers cover her lips and she felt the instant response of her body.

'—at the end of my stay here,' he said softly, a trace of mockery gleaming in his eyes as he finished his sentence. 'Once a year I am given the chance to be alone. I will not relinquish that luxury for anyone. I will *not* change my plans for a woman.'

Bella made a sound in her throat but his fingers still covered her lips.

'Which gives you two choices.' He spoke in a deceptively gentle voice. 'Either you can try and make your own way on foot—and if you do that I calculate you'll be dead in an hour or so—or you stay here with me until it suits me to return you to Al-Rafid.'

CHAPTER THREE

ZAFIQ withdrew his hand from her lips, fighting an inexplicable temptation to replace it with his mouth. 'Those are your options. Pick one.'

Anger flared inside him but the anger was directed towards himself and his own weakness.

Despite her ordeal, she was more alluring than any other woman he'd ever encountered, and his jaw tightened because she was a woman who knew how to use her gifts and he despised the fact that he was susceptible to her practised flirtation.

The rigid self-control and discipline on which he prided himself suddenly seemed like a flimsy, fragile thing. It was like going into battle and discovering that your armour was made of paper.

Perhaps, he mused grimly, *he'd never been really tested before.*

Was that what this week of reflection and personal time was going to be about? His own weakness?

Was he about to discover that he was, after all, just like his father?

His initial suspicions that she was part of the conspiracy to steal his horse had been eliminated by her explanation. It was galling to acknowledge that he might actually have to be grateful to her because it seemed that she'd inadvertently foiled a serious crime. By 'borrowing' Amira she had clearly prevented the threatened kidnap by a matter of minutes. Contemplating the reaction of the criminals who had been planning to steal his horse, he gave a grim smile. They must have had a shock to discover that someone had already done the job for them.

He was determined to keep his precious mare safe in his care until he was due to return to the city.

Which meant keeping the girl too.

Zafiq watched as various emotions flickered across her beautiful face.

Even with sand in her golden hair she was gorgeous. She reminded him of a princess from one of the fairy stories he'd read to his younger sisters when they were small. Only less sweet natured. *A sulky princess.* Now that he'd thwarted her plans to escape from the desert, he could see her struggling to hold back her temper. She was fiery and full of fight and he wondered what she was hiding.

Her hands clenched and she glared at him. 'Don't put yourself out, will you?'

Accustomed to receiving the appropriate degree of respect at all times, Zafiq was taken aback by her lack of deference. 'Generally people put themselves out for me,' he drawled softly. 'That's the way it works.'

'You say "jump" and they say "how high?"'

'Something like that.'

She tilted her head and studied him with perfect blue eyes that had undoubtedly been designed by nature to bring a man to his knees. 'If that's how you expect people to behave around you, then you definitely don't want to keep me here. I'm honestly not great at doing as I'm told. In fact, I'm rubbish. That's why I've been banished to the middle of the desert. I'll drive you mad if you make me stay.'

Zafiq almost laughed.

She was already driving him mad, but he had no intention of revealing that.

'You seem anxious to become better acquainted with the inside of a prison cell.' His remark appeared to register because her face coloured.

'Look, I know it was wrong to take the horse, OK? But—'

'Not for taking the horse.' Reluctant to reveal that he was actually grateful to her for that part of her escapade, Zafiq trod with caution. 'For speaking to me with such a lack of respect.'

'At least prison has bars, which would be a step up from the Retreat,' she quipped, quickly regaining her spirit. 'Alcohol is banned. You have to get your highs from herbal tea.' She studied his reaction and then rolled her eyes. 'I liked you better when you laughed. You should do it more often.' Tense and edgy, she paced to the other side of the tent. 'What am I supposed to call you, then?'

'Your Highness.'

'Wow. No formality, then! And I'm supposed to do everything you tell me, *Your Highness*?' Her mouth curved into a mocking smile that challenged his already straining self-control. 'So I'm your slave, is that right? Sorry, I should have said, *Is that right, Your Highness*?'

Zafiq had a disturbing image of this blonde, defiant beauty dressed in thin veils and bound at the wrists and ankles, awaiting his pleasure. 'I hadn't considered that option, but I will bear it in mind.'

His reply seemed to unsettle her. The dangerous gleam in her sexy eyes was almost enough to make Zafiq rethink his ultimatum.

She was the most alluring, tempting woman he'd ever met.

'We will get along very well together,' he said in a cool tone. 'As long as you obey certain basic rules.'

'And what are those?' She flicked her hair out of her eyes in an unconsciously graceful gesture. 'I just have to do everything you say, *Your Highness*?'

'Yes.' He watched as she swayed slightly and suddenly he remembered how long she'd been exposed to the sun. She must be feeling awful and yet she was determined to hide it from him and it was impossible not to admire that. 'You're still suffering from dehydration. Drink something.'

'You might be a sheikh, but could you stop ordering me around? It brings out the worst in me.' But she sank back onto the mattress and reached for the glass, her hand shaking as she sipped the water. 'I feel filthy. My hair is full of sand. Does this tent have an en-suite bathroom or anything?'

For some reason he found her sense of humour every bit as disturbing as her more obvious charms. People were usually stilted and formal around him. They didn't crack jokes. 'As it happens, there is an en-suite bathroom. Outside the tent. This is an oasis. There's a pool.'

'I hope it's an infinity pool with a bar serving iced drinks in the corner and a changing room. Or am I supposed to strip off in public?'

'It's not public. I'm the only person here.'

'Well…' She took another sip of water and then put the glass down. 'In that case, no peeping. And what about the creatures you mentioned before? Am I likely to be eaten while I'm bathing?'

He refrained from admitting that she was probably the most dangerous creature in the area. 'I doubt you'll be eaten.'

'Good, because I don't have a particular desire to be tonight's takeaway for some hungry camel.'

'Camels are herbivores.'

She shuddered and lifted her hands, palms towards him like a stop sign, but there was a twinkle of mischief in those eyes. '*Don't* mention herbs to me again—after a week at the Retreat, I never want to hear about herbs again. I don't want to eat them, and I don't want to drink them.' Her cheeks dimpled and a smile burst across her face like the sun emerging from behind a cloud. 'And I don't want to ride on one either. If there's herb in the word, count me out. I suppose it's useless to ask if you have a change of clothes? Mirror? Hairdryer?'

'Wash your clothes in the oasis.' He was irritated by how much that smile affected him. 'They'll dry quickly if you put them on a rock.'

'And in the meantime I'm supposed to walk around naked?'

'In the meantime you wear a robe.' It might be a good for his sanity, Zafiq thought grimly, to cover her up from head to foot. The mere mention of the word *naked* was enough to make him consider jumping back in the pool himself simply for its cooling effects on his overtaxed libido. 'And stay out of the sun.'

Bella sank under the still surface of the water. Her skin was burning from the sun exposure; she felt hot, grubby and unattractive but she *did* feel better now that she'd cooled off, and it was bliss to wash off the sand that appeared to have stuck to every part of her skin. There was no mirror in the tent but the Sheikh's indifference to her as a woman told her everything she needed to know.

Clearly she looked a complete fright. Like some sort of alien sand monster. If she'd been thinking clearly she would have bathed in the pool before trying to talk him into taking her to the city.

Still unable to believe that he was going to make her stay here with him, she glared at the outside of the large white tent.

Where was he anyway? Meditating?

Bella frowned as she tried to see her reflection in the water.

No, a man with muscles like that had to do something more physical than meditate.

Was he watching her?

The thought made her shiver and she dipped under the water again and did her best to remove the sand from her hair, methodically working on it section by section.

'Never again am I taking shampoo for granted.' Despite her disappointment at not being back in the city, she had to admit that the pool was beautiful. Shaded by palm trees, the calm, glassy surface of the water reflected the perfectly blue sky, and beyond the palm trees the dunes rose steeply, turned to a shade of pinky orange by the late-afternoon sun.

It wasn't the city, but it was better than being trapped in the Retreat. Better than having to meditate or contemplate or whatever, Bella mused as she cleansed the last section of her hair and then turned onto her back. Floating in the peaceful pool, staring up at the sky, she felt unusually tranquil.

In fact, the whole situation was surprisingly relaxing.

The Sheikh had no idea who she really was. He knew nothing of the latest Balfour scandal. They'd probably never even heard of the Balfours out here in the desert.

Which suited her perfectly.

Although she'd hated the Retreat, Bella knew she couldn't go home.

What was there to go home for?

They didn't want her there.

She'd made a hideous mess of her life.

Feeling tears prick her eyes, Bella dipped her head under the water, feeling more alone than she'd ever felt.

Feeling the water ripple around her she spluttered to the surface, realising that she wasn't as alone as she'd thought.

The Sheikh's stallion stood on the edge of the oasis, drinking from the water.

'Hi, there.' Bella grinned at him, admiring the powerful muscles of his neck and legs. 'Are you really as dangerous as he says you are? You don't look it.'

At the sound of her voice, the horse reared up, showing the whites of his eyes as he pawed the air.

'All right, I get the message,' Bella said drily, 'you're dangerous. And moody like your master. Calm down, will you? I'm harmless.' She swam across from the centre of the pool and swept her dripping hair out of her eyes. 'What else can you do? Any other tricks?'

The horse flattened his ears to his head and stared at her suspiciously.

Bella was about to reach out her hand to stroke him when a masculine voice stopped her.

'Don't touch him—he has a very uncertain temper. He could hurt you.'

Bella froze, but the sudden tremor of her limbs wasn't caused by fear of the horse. 'Have you been watching me?'

'I was watching the pool. As you seem to have the most astonishing propensity for attracting trouble, I thought it might be the simplest way to keep you alive.'

'I'm not your responsibility.'

'I know. But if you die out here in the desert I will have to take your body back to the city and that doesn't fit in with my plans.'

'Oh, thanks!' Her tone sarcastic, Bella waded

into shallower water, forgetting that she was naked from the waist up.

She heard his sudden indrawn breath and saw his gaze linger on her body in an unmistakably masculine appraisal.

Bella resisted the inexplicable urge to cover herself. 'Stop staring.'

'If you didn't want me to look, you wouldn't have removed your clothes.'

'I only have one set,' she said tartly. 'It's either naked in the water, or naked all evening. Take your pick.'

'You have no modesty.'

'If you don't like it, don't look, Your Highness.' But she saw the unmistakable gleam of admiration in his eyes as he scanned her curves reluctantly. Reluctant was good, she told herself. Reluctant meant the emotion he was feeling was more powerful than he wanted it to be. And there was no better confidence booster than a man who wanted her despite himself. Starved of affection—*deeply wounded by the rejection of her family*—Bella couldn't help enjoying that admiration.

She stepped out of the water and twisted her hair into a thick rope, squeezing out the water, not bothering to cover herself. Although she didn't look at the Sheikh, she was hyperaware of him as she stretched out her hand to the snorting stallion.

She could feel him looking at her.

'You need to calm down,' she cooed. 'There's no need to be all macho and dominating. I know you're stronger than I am.' She talked to the animal in a low voice and the horse blew through his nostrils, watching her all the time.

His head snaked forward in a rapid movement and in an instant the Sheikh was between her and the horse.

Controlling the stallion with a single, abrupt command, he closed his hand round Bella's wrist and dragged her towards the tent.

'You are the most provoking, wilful, obstinate—'

'Irresponsible, thoughtless, selfish,' Bella added helpfully, and he growled deep in his throat and hauled her against his hard, powerful body. Without hesitation or warning he brought his mouth down on hers and she felt his strong hands slide down her bare back, holding her captive. Her damp skin burned against the pressure of his fingers and sexual excitement consumed her body like a ravenous beast.

As his mouth plundered hers with raw, unrestrained passion all she was aware of was heat.

The heat of his tongue, the heat of the tent and the scorching heat that seared through her body like a flaming lance.

It was like nothing she'd ever felt before.

Like nothing she'd ever imagined—

And then he released her, thrusting her away from him as if she were infectious.

Suddenly unsupported, Bella swayed, dizzy and disorientated from his kiss and wondering why he would want to stop doing something that felt so good.

Up until that point in her life if anyone had asked her if she'd ever been kissed, she would have said yes. Only now did she realise that she would have been lying.

She'd never been kissed.

Not like that.

Everything that had happened to her before this moment had been a pale imitation of the real thing.

Where had he learned to kiss a woman like that?

'Cover yourself!' His voice harsh, he kept his back to her and Bella stared blankly at his wide shoulders, wondering why he was so angry. She was feeling a thousand different emotions, but anger certainly wasn't one of them.

But she didn't argue. She saw the white robe that he'd spread on the bed, picked it up and slipped it over her head. It fell to the ground and she pulled a face.

'Great. Right on trend. Do you have a pair of scissors or something? I'm going to break my neck if I wander around in this.' She was surprised that her voice sounded so normal, because inside she felt anything but normal. That kiss had left her feeling as though she'd been mixed in a cocktail shaker.

He turned swiftly, his dark eyes hooded, his mouth a firm, uncompromising line as he swept her appearance in a single glance. Without saying a word he took the dagger from the folds of his robe and stepped towards her.

Alarmed, Bella took an involuntary step backwards. 'There's no need to— Oh—' She squeaked in astonishment as he bent down, sliced the blade through the fabric and removed the surplus material in two bold strokes. The robe now stopped just above the ankle and Bella stared at his dark, glossy hair, heart thumping.

'So the blade isn't ornamental, then,' she croaked, and he straightened in a lithe movement, his eyes menacing.

'No.' He slid it back inside his robe. 'It isn't.'

She licked her lips. 'Why do you carry a knife?'

Without bothering to answer her question he strode out of the tent, leaving her staring after him, wondering what she'd done wrong.

He'd kissed *her*, hadn't he? Surely he couldn't blame her for that.

Irritated by the injustice of it all, Bella sat down on the bed, touching her lips with her fingers. Her lips were so dry after her day in the desert, it must have been like kissing sandpaper.

Feeling more vulnerable than she wanted to admit, she combed her fingers through her rapidly drying hair, wishing she could do something about her appearance.

There must be *something* she could use to see her reflection.

Typical, she thought gloomily. She met the man of her dreams and she didn't even have a mirror or a decent pair of shoes.

No wonder he'd virtually run out of the tent. He'd probably prefer to look at his horse.

Bella's wounded pride made her reluctant to leave the tent, but her restless nature made it impossible for her to sit still for long. And she couldn't quite believe that he'd knocked her back.

She was used to fending men off, not chasing after them.

Telling herself that if he didn't want to look at her, then he could face the opposite direction, Bella stalked out of the tent.

The throb in her head was growing steadily worse again but she was too proud to ask if he had any tablets.

'I have made you tea.' His deep voice came from a few metres away and she turned to look at him, noticing that he'd built a fire.

'If it's herbal tea, I might just have to kill you.' Bella rubbed her hands up her arms, wondering how it was possible to feel shivery in the desert. 'I don't suppose you have anything more interesting to drink? Champagne?'

He didn't smile. 'It's Bedouin tea.'

'What's Bedouin tea? Tea you drink before you go to bed?' Still cross with him, she knelt down gingerly on the rug he'd placed on the sand, determined not to show how bad she felt.

'It's made from tea leaf, sugar and desert herbs—' He poured some of the dark liquid into a cup and handed it to her. 'It has a very distinctive flavour. Try it.'

'I've drunk more tea in the past two weeks than I've had in my whole life.' Bella sniffed the tea cautiously, took a sip and wrinkled her nose. 'It tastes…different. I hadn't imagined you drinking tea—'

'It is customary to drink tea with a guest and share stories and news. The Bedouin are very hospitable people. And excellent story tellers.'

'So tell me a story. But make sure it has a happy ending. No drama or misery. A few fairy princesses wouldn't go amiss.' She'd had more than enough drama lately to last her a lifetime. 'Tell me about the Bedouin. They're nomadic, aren't they? So are you rediscovering your tribal roots?'

'The sheikh is basically the leader of the tribe.'

'All-powerful. Do people shake when they see you coming? Get it? Shake…sheikh…?' Her voice trailed off. She grinned at him, her hands curled round the mug, eyeing the austere lines of his handsome face. 'You don't smile much, do you?'

'I smile when I'm amused.'

Refusing to be daunted, Bella blew gently on her tea. 'You need to lighten up and take life less seriously.'

'Perhaps you need to take it *more* seriously. Then you wouldn't find yourself dying of heatstroke and thirst, or stranded alone in the desert with a stranger.'

'So what amuses you? You said you smile when you're amused. So I'm wondering what makes you laugh. Obviously not my appalling sheikh jokes.' She took another sip of tea and decided that the taste was growing on her. 'When was the last time you collapsed with laughter? You know, laughed so hard you couldn't speak—laughed so hard you almost cracked a rib.'

The fire crackled and a whisper of smoke curled into the air. 'I can't recall ever having "collapsed with laughter" and amusement has never affected my ability to converse.'

'Don't people ever make jokes around you?'

'Never.'

'Because you're so intimidating, I suppose.' Seriously worried by how ill she felt, Bella curled her legs to one side. 'What do you do to relax, then? Parties? Do you *sheikh* rock and roll?'

A muscle flickered in his lean, angular jaw. 'You just can't help yourself, can you?'

'No. I can't. Sorry. I'm trying to make you laugh but I know when I'm beaten, Your Highness,' Bella said flippantly, really disconcerted by the fact he hadn't smiled at a single one of her jokes.

Used to being the centre of attention wherever she went, she didn't know how to react to him.

He added something to the food bubbling in the pot. 'Presumably you frequently collapse with laughter?'

'Quite often. Usually at awkward times. There's something about stiff, formal occasions that makes me want to giggle. Usually at about the same moment someone is pointing a camera at me.'

His glance was penetrating. 'You attend many stiff, formal occasions with photographers in attendance?'

Bella stilled. 'Not really. Church and stuff. Family photographs.' *The annual Balfour Ball with shoals of hungry paparazzi ready to indulge in a feeding frenzy.*

Thinking of that particular event wiped the desire to laugh from her body.

He was still watching her. 'Is everything a joke to you?'

'No,' Bella said flatly, staring down at her empty mug and trying not to think about the latest scandal she'd unearthed. 'But I prefer to try and see the funny side of life whenever possible.'

'You are extremely frivolous.'

'Yeah, that's me.' Her voice husky, Bella kept

her eyes fixed on the mug until she was sure she was in control. 'You ought to meet my father. You'd get on really well. If you have a spare month you could compare notes on my deficiencies. So you're from a noble family, is that right? How come you speak perfect English?'

'I went to a boarding school in England. My father understood the importance of maintaining our unique history and culture whilst incorporating the advances of the modern world.'

Bella looked around her, surprised to realise that it had grown dark while they were talking. Above them what seemed like a million tiny silver stars gleamed in a cloudless desert sky and she stared up at them in fascination. 'I feel as though I could reach out and touch them. I don't remember there being this many stars in England.'

'You have too much light pollution.'

Or maybe she'd never stopped to look at the sky. 'It's pretty. Reminds me of a dress I had once—' she tilted her head to one side '—indigo silk with tiny silver beads.'

'Do you ever think of anything other than how you look?'

'Looking good is part of my job,' Bella said defensively and then flushed as his eyes narrowed.

'What is your job?'

'Oh, this and that...' She was tempted to just say 'doctor' or 'lawyer' or something that would wipe the arrogant look off his face. She didn't think he'd be impressed to know she spent most of her day asleep and most of the night at parties, wearing clothes by designers who were desperate to have their creations modelled by Bella Balfour. 'I'm sort of in between jobs at the moment.'

'It is good to take time out to reflect on how you are spending your life. Everyone needs time to think about whether they are making a difference.'

'Absolutely.' Bella squirmed, pretty sure that she didn't make a difference to anyone. At least, not a positive one. 'Is that why you're here?'

'I spend a week in the desert to escape the constant pressures of twenty-first-century life.'

'Don't you miss civilization? How do you survive without the Internet?'

'The Internet is a useful tool, not an addiction.'

'For me it's an addiction. I'm a Google girl. How do you stop yourself playing around with it?' Bella waved her hand and then remembered that she hadn't had a manicure for two weeks and tucked it out of sight. 'I go on to look up one thing—I don't know, let's say a new spa or something—next thing I know, an hour has passed and I haven't done the thing I was supposed to do. I'm horribly undisciplined.'

'I have no trouble believing that.'

She looked at the pot on the fire. 'So if you've gone back to nature, how did you light the fire? Did you rub two sticks together? Use a magnifying glass to concentrate the sun's rays?'

'I used a match,' he said drily and Bella giggled and wagged her finger at him.

'That's a disgraceful short cut. I'm really disappointed in you. You should have been setting fire to camel dung at the very least.' She was painfully conscious of him—of his strength and competence. 'But you enjoy being away from everything, honestly?'

'Desert life is hard, but simple. The problems are basic ones that man has faced for centuries. Where to find food and water. How to provide for a family. I enjoy the silence and I enjoy being with the horses.'

'How come the stallion is happy alongside the mare?'

'They know each other well.'

'So the mare I took, you know her?'

'Amira—she belongs to me.'

Bella remembered the guards. '*You* own those stables?'

'You ask too many questions.' He poured more tea into her mug and spooned food into a bowl. 'Eat. You haven't eaten all day.'

She stared at the bowl he handed her. 'You cook for yourself?'

'Is that so surprising?'

Bella put her mug on the ground and lifted the bowl, realising that she was expected to eat with her fingers. 'Well, you don't exactly come across as "new man," if that's what you're asking me. I suppose I expected you to have chefs and people running round after you.' Examining the contents, she tried to imagine her father or any of the men she knew cooking anywhere, let alone the desert. 'I'm impressed. I think.' She sniffed suspiciously. 'What is it? Camel stew? Loin of lizard?'

'It's rice and vegetables.'

Stung by his tone, Bella tightened her grip on the bowl. 'You think I'm a complete waste of space, don't you?'

'I am trying *not* to think about you.' He kept his eyes on the fire as he ate his meal, the fire illuminating his handsome face. 'This is not how I envisaged my few days in the desert. It is supposed to be time for contemplation. And relaxation. Clearly you know nothing of either pastime.'

'That's not fair! I'm not stopping you relaxing.'

A sardonic smile touched his beautiful mouth. 'You think not, *habibiti*?'

Her insides decidedly unsettled, Bella sampled the stew gingerly. 'This tastes good. I'm not going to get in your way, I promise. Just do what you would normally do if I weren't here.'

'I am.' He ladled more stew into his own bowl. 'Unfortunately you are doing it with me.'

'Ignore me.'

'How do you propose I do that? You are not an easy woman to ignore.'

His words sent a thrill of excitement through her body. 'No?'

'A woman as beautiful as you cannot fail to know precisely what effect she has on men.'

'You don't seem to be having too much trouble resisting me.'

'I have a severe aversion to being manipulated. Every look you give me and every word you speak is a carefully constructed plan to get your own way.'

Bella was starting to feel truly dreadful. The shivering intensified by the moment and her head throbbed too badly to allow her to construct a smart response. She wished she hadn't eaten. 'All right. I'll stop talking.'

'Is that truly a possibility?' The irony in his tone was matched by the gleam in his eyes. 'You strike me as a woman who has never learned the meaning of the word *silence*.'

His harsh evaluation was all the more hurtful because she was feeling so ill. Suddenly she felt horribly vulnerable, alone in the desert with this ice-cold stranger.

She ought to be putting all her efforts into persuading him to take her to the city, but she felt too ill to summon up the energy.

It was only when the bowl was gently removed from her hands that she realised that he was watching her.

'I'm fine,' she whispered fiercely, and he sighed.

'Go to bed. Tomorrow you will feel better.'

Would she? She didn't think she'd ever feel better again. Despite the fire, her teeth were chattering. 'I—is it c-cold or is it me? Do you have a j-jumper or something?'

With a driven sigh, he rose to his feet. 'You have sunstroke—that is why you are shivering.'

'Sunstroke? That sounds serious!' Alarmed,

Bella stared at him, her teeth still clattering. 'Sh-should you call an air ambulance or something?'

'There are no emergency services in the desert.'

'I d-don't want to d-die in the d-desert.'

'That is unlikely.'

'And I b-bet you're disappointed about that.'

'Can you walk back to the tent or do you want me to carry you?'

'I don't want you to touch me!'

'Good—' His mouth grim, he doused the fire. 'On that one thing, at least, we are in agreement. You need to go to bed and rest. Keep drinking. I will bring you a blanket and some cream for your skin.'

Feeling wretched, Bella dragged herself into the tent and collapsed on the bed. 'At least this ultrastylish garment you've given me to wear can pass as nightwear.'

A look of exasperation on his handsome face, he tucked a blanket over her. But despite his rough tone his fingers were gentle as he checked the temperature of her forehead. 'Sleep. You will be better by tomorrow.'

Still shivering, Bella closed her eyes. 'And then what?'

'You and I are going to have to learn to live alongside each other, *habibiti*.' He gave a humourless laugh. 'Unless you develop a sudden gift for silence, I suspect that will prove a challenge.'

CHAPTER FOUR

ZAFIQ urged his stallion across the sand, his hands barely touching the reins. Usually on his first night in the desert he fell into a soundless, dreamless sleep. Last night, sleep had eluded him and he'd stared at the stars for more hours than he cared to remember.

And the reason for his unusual bout of insomnia was currently asleep in the tent.

His tent.

Concerned about the shivering, he'd checked on her several times during the night and watching her sleep had proved every bit as disturbing as spending time with her awake. Asleep she lost the feisty, wilful side that was so much a part of her personality. Instead she looked vulnerable, her incredible blonde hair trailing over the sheets and her body curled into a fetal position, as if she were trying to protect herself.

Wiping that memory from his brain, Zafiq urged Batal faster. Usually, riding was guaran-teed to clear his mind but apparently the golden-haired goddess had the ability to ruin even that simple pleasure.

Even a swim in the oasis hadn't cooled his blood because his memory of her walking semi-naked through the water was indelibly printed on his brain.

Temptation, he thought grimly, *had been shaped into the form of a woman.*

Was this what his father had faced with his stepmother? All those times he'd given in to her greedy demands, was this what he had been fighting?

For the first time Zafiq felt a flicker of sympathy towards his father and then he crushed it.

A man always had a choice, he reminded himself grimly, no matter how captivating the woman. And the true test of a man lay in the choices he made, not when those choices were easy, but when he was presented with temptation.

And he would *not* be making the same choices as his father.

He would *never* allow his judgement to be clouded by his feelings for a woman.

It wasn't even as if she was his type of woman. She showed neither respect nor modesty. Accustomed to women who were usually overwhelmed to meet him in person, Zafiq found her vitality and lack of deference disconcerting to say the least.

Today he would urge her to remain inside the tent, away from the harsh desert sun. And he'd make sure she didn't remove her robe again during their time in the desert. If she had to stay, then she had to learn to behave, he thought savagely, shielding his eyes against the sun as he focused on the horizon.

Having formulated what he believed to be a workable solution to the problem, Zafiq rode back to the desert camp, confident that he had his emotions well in hand.

Suddenly Batal gave a shriek of anger and rose on his hind legs, sawing at the air with his hooves. Welded to the back of the plunging animal, Zafiq spoke to the horse quietly, using all his strength to hold the powerful stallion in check.

Only when he'd calmed Batal did he look to see what had spooked him.

She stood in the shadow of the tent, her hair damp from another cooling dip in the oasis.

'Sorry, I didn't know you were out on the horse. You startled me.' The redness of her skin had calmed overnight and her beautiful face now had a healthy glow.

But what really caught his attention was the way she was dressed.

For the first time in his life Zafiq found it difficult to speak. 'What have you done to the robe?'

'I altered it a bit.' She glanced down at herself, her blonde hair sliding forward in a silken mass of temptation. 'It was too long.'

'It was a perfect length,' Zafiq ground out, and she looked up at him with a stunning smile, her eyes challenging him to a fight.

'If this is offending you, you could always take me to the city.'

So that was her plan.

She was trying to drive him mad.

And she was succeeding.

Rigid in the saddle, Zafiq scanned her outfit in silent disbelief.

Somehow she'd turned a modest, shapeless robe into a high-fashion item.

She'd ripped the fabric with her hands, tearing a metre off the bottom so that it now skimmed her thighs, exposing her incredible legs. And, as if that wasn't bad enough, she'd taken some of the leaves from a date palm and woven them into a belt, accentuating her tiny waist.

Suffering from an explosive blast of sexual

arousal, Zafiq took a deep breath and acknowledged that his plan to cover her up had failed spectacularly.

She looked like a temptress straight from a Greek myth.

Frustrated by his own response, he raked his brain for an alternative solution to concealing her. 'You will stay in the tent today,' he commanded, and she raised her eyebrows, a hint of humour in her gorgeous blue eyes.

'Am I supposed to say, "Yes, Your Highness"?'

'"Yes, Your Highness" would be fine.'

Her smile was apologetic. 'Trouble is, I've never been much good at doing what people want me to do. I was brought up to challenge and question. I have a tendency to do the opposite of what I'm asked.'

Zafiq's gaze didn't shift. 'In that case, I order you to stay out of the tent and to walk around half naked until we leave this place.'

She collapsed into a fit of giggles, her laughter so infectious that he felt the corners of his mouth twitch.

'You see?' She was still grinning, a tiny dimple flickering at the corner of her full mouth. 'You *do* have a sense of humour. You're smiling.'

Was he? Zafiq vaulted from the horse, removed

the animal's bridle and urged him towards the oasis to drink, reminding himself that there was *nothing* amusing about this situation. But he had to admit that there was something incredibly refreshing about being with someone who didn't automatically say what they thought he wanted to hear. 'How is your headache?'

'Gone, thanks. Did you get any sleep on the floor? Must have been pretty uncomfortable.'

'I slept,' he lied, unwilling to admit even to himself that this woman would cause him a moment of unbroken sleep. 'Are you ready for breakfast?'

'Definitely. I'm starving. Then I think I might go for a swim—naked, of course—and then a long ride in the desert—'

'You are being intentionally provoking—'

'No, I'm being me. And you don't like me, so why don't you just take me to the city? Then you can have a few days' peace and quiet. I'm nothing but trouble.'

'The ability to handle trouble is the true test of a man's character,' Zafiq purred, and watched with satisfaction as a flicker of surprise touched her beautiful face. 'And I love being tested.'

He had no intention of revealing that he'd never been tested like this before.

Never before had he felt such a powerful urge to forget who he was and just lose himself with a beautiful woman.

Irritated by his own thoughts, Zafiq scanned her slender frame. 'You don't look like a woman who eats breakfast.'

'I burn off a lot of calories.' She sounded defensive, as if he wasn't the first person to say that to her. 'There's nothing wrong with me, OK? I don't have an eating disorder and I'm not on any stupid diet—'

'Is that what people say about you?'

'No.' Her denial was a little too fast. 'Anyway, I don't care what people say. I'm slender because I'm a very physical person.'

Zafiq closed his eyes briefly, trying to dispel the image her words created. Everything about her was bold, physical and athletic, from the long limbs clearly displayed under the remodelled robe to the strength in her slender arms. She was vibrant, energetic and *alive.*

'I'm hot after my ride. I'm going to bathe.' His jaw clenched, Zafiq strode towards the tent and then paused and delivered a warning glare. 'And I *don't* want an audience.'

'OK, Your Highness.' The dimple was back. 'I promise not to peep.'

Growling deep in his throat, Zafiq took refuge in the tent.

She was slowly driving him mad.

Reviewing the success of her plan with delight, Bella sat in the shade of a large date palm, fanning herself with a giant leaf. At this rate she'd be back in the city by lunchtime.

Lying there in the oppressive heat, she realised that the knot of tension in her stomach had eased and that she actually felt rested for the first time in two weeks. Last night she'd slept. No bad dreams.

Brushing an insect off her arm, Bella wondered why. She was still in the desert. She still had all the problems that had been with her when she'd arrived two weeks earlier. What had changed?

Hearing a splash, she stopped fanning herself and watched as the Sheikh powered through the water with rhythmic strokes, the muscles across his shoulders rippling as he swam.

He was fit, she thought dreamily, in more ways than one.

And he was going to go mad when he saw her sitting here.

Whether he'd be angry enough to banish her somewhere civilised remained to be seen.

How long would it take her to get her own way? Hopefully after a morning in her company, he'd be calling the cavalry and expelling her to civilisation.

In the meantime, she was going to enjoy herself. How often did she get the chance to admire a physique like his?

He was, without doubt, the sexiest man she'd ever encountered.

Bella rested her chin on her hands, her eyes following every movement of his bronzed, hard body as he put himself through a punishing physical workout. He was the polar opposite of the pale, artistic society types she mixed with. Not just in looks, but in personality and behaviour.

And then there was the fact that he was so serious.

Bella gave a little frown.

Not her type.

So why was she sitting here watching him?

What she should really be doing was making the best of herself, but it was hard to make the best of yourself without a mirror.

She stared at his discarded robe and suddenly she had an idea.

Glancing across the water to check he still had

his back to her, she leant across and picked up the robe, retrieving the knife gingerly.

The deadly blade glinted in the harsh overhead sun and Bella smiled as she tilted it to find the right angle.

'What are you doing there?'

Caught out, Bella glanced up guiltily and saw the anger flash across his face. Ignoring her thundering pulse rate, she smiled sweetly, raising her voice so that he could hear. 'Er, fiddling with your dagger and watching you?'

Instead of replying he swam back towards her, each stroke a study in controlled, masculine power.

Remembering that kiss, her heart started to thud and she felt an almost ridiculous urge to make a run for it. But her limbs wouldn't move so she stayed as she was, sitting in the dust, her eyes on the man, the dagger clutched in her hand.

He emerged from the pool like some glorious vision of athletic perfection, water pouring off his muscular frame, his abdomen flat and strong, his chest and legs shaded by dark hairs.

Bella tried to say something flippant but discovered she wasn't capable of saying anything at all when confronted by such raw masculinity.

Raking his dripping hair away from his face,

he stared at her angrily. 'You were *not* supposed to be watching me.'

'There's nothing else to do. I don't have a laptop, a cellphone or an iPod.'

'And without those you cannot occupy yourself? You rely on technology for entertainment?'

'Yes, I do. It's how I keep in touch with my friends. I can't do that, so I thought I'd watch you instead.'

'I am not your friend.'

'No, but you're a living creature, which is a start. And you're pretty good to look at.' She knew she was playing a dangerous game, but she was desperate for him to take her back to the city and she was pretty sure that he'd crack eventually.

'You are intentionally provocative.' Without waiting for her response, he removed the knife from her hand and hauled her to her feet, his furious dark eyes only centimetres from hers as he yanked her against him. 'What were you planning to do with the knife?'

'Calm down, will you?' Bella bit back a gasp as her thigh brushed against his. 'I was going to use it as a mirror.'

'A *mirror*?'

'Yes, the blade is shiny…metal—I've been trapped without a mirror for two weeks! I just wanted to know whether the damage can ever be repaired.'

He glanced down at the lethal blade in his hand in astonishment as if its alternative properties had never occurred to him before. 'A mirror—'

'Look,' Bella snapped, 'the desert may be heaven to you, but to me it's the opposite, OK? I can't do any of the things I normally do!'

'You spend your day looking in the mirror?'

Feeling shallow, Bella shrank slightly. 'Try being me before you pass judgement,' she muttered. 'If I leave the house without make-up, everyone is suddenly asking whether I'm ill, or on drugs, or about to be admitted to a clinic. Whatever I wear is scrutinised—people are *mean*.'

'*Who* is mean?'

Recovering from the shocking fact that she'd actually admitted to someone how much the negative press coverage actually hurt her feelings, Bella backtracked. 'Friends,' she said vaguely, 'and family—'

'Your friends and family scrutinise everything you wear? They're mean?'

'Oh, whatever—' Realising that she was digging a hole for herself, Bella shrugged. 'It doesn't matter. I'm just saying it's second nature for me to look in a mirror and just check I haven't woken up with a huge spot on my nose.'

'And what do you do if you have?'

'I stay indoors.'

'Your life is truly bizarre.'

Bella frowned. She'd lived that life for so long she no longer even questioned it. *Was it bizarre?*

He gave an impatient sigh. 'You need to stop thinking about the way you look and learn humility. And obedience. I told you not to sit there and watch. Don't challenge me, *habibiti*, because you will *not* win.'

'Oh, dear, am I annoying you?' She forced the taunt past dry, stiff lips and saw the flare of anger in the depths of his gaze.

'Yes,' he gritted, his hand tightening around her wrist, 'but my response to that will not be to send you away, but to keep you closer. Remember that, before you push me too far, Kate.'

Kate? Who on earth was Kate? Bella opened her mouth to tell him that he ought to at least get her name right and then remembered that *she* was the one who had introduced herself as Kate.

Out here in the burning sands of the desert, Bella Balfour didn't exist.

What a confusing mess she'd created, although

there *was* something liberating about being anonymous. It would be even better if she could be anonymous somewhere with decent facilities.

'Why would you keep me closer if I'm annoying?'

His smile was lethal. 'Because I intend to teach you how to behave. You need to learn respect.'

'What are you going to do? Throw me over your knee?' Bella's tone was sassy but her heart was thudding. 'This is the twenty-first century.'

'You are in the desert. Here, time has stood still. And since you are so determined to watch me in the water, you can join me.' Without warning, he swept her off her feet and dropped her into the water.

Unprepared, Bella sank under the surface, the water closing over her head. For a moment everything was muted and she kicked frantically, swallowed several mouthfuls before she surfaced, coughing, only to find him in the pool next to her. Sweeping her sodden hair away from her face, she took a gulp of air.

'Are you trying to drown me?' She coughed again and thumped her chest with her hand, trying to clear the water from her lungs. 'Why did you do that?'

'I thought you needed cooling down.' A sardonic

smile on his face, he swam away from her, leaving Bella staring after him.

Filling her lungs with air, she ducked under the water and followed him across the pool, making sure she was deep enough not to create a ripple on the surface.

Where was he?

She peered through the murky grey-green water, wishing she had swimming goggles, and then saw a pair of strong male legs directly in front of her.

Smiling, Bella silently ducked to the bottom of the pool, intending to grab his foot and unbalance him, but a large hand caught her shoulder and hauled her to the surface.

'You can swim.'

'Were you hoping I'd drown?' Grumpy that he'd seen her, Bella fought to catch her breath. 'How did you know I was there?'

'Because your behaviour is extremely predictable. It's designed to cause maximum irritation.'

'You think I'm predictable?'

'Kate, you do whatever you can to be as annoying as possible. Are you afraid of wildlife? Because there is plenty in this pool.'

'Is that what women do around you? Squeal and

come over all girly? I hate to remove the opportunity for you to play macho man, but I can lift spiders from the bath without help.' Bella twisted her hair into a rope, wringing out the water. 'If you want a screaming maiden, you're looking at the wrong woman. I tell you what—I'll race you across the pool. If I win, you take me back to the city.'

His eyes darkened. 'I will *not* race a woman.'

'Why? Because you might lose? Don't worry, Your Highness. I promise not to tell anyone when I beat you.'

He stared at her in incredulous silence and then he shook his head and started to laugh. Transfixed by the change in him, Bella's own smile faded.

Moody, he was incredibly handsome but when he smiled… Oh, no, no, no—

Her limbs felt weak and suddenly she was thinking about that kiss.

About his wickedly clever mouth…

This is *not* good, Bella thought uneasily, trying to ignore the heat spreading through her body. Finding a total chauvinist so shockingly attractive was incredibly embarrassing. Not something you'd ever admit in public. Still, at least no one she knew was around to see her temporary lapse in taste and judgement.

'Watching her, he lifted an eyebrow. 'Now what? No smart remark?'

Arrogance just wasn't attractive, Bella told herself firmly. 'I'm just psyching myself up to beat you. I hope you're a good loser.'

'I wouldn't know.' A sardonic smile touched his beautiful mouth. 'I've never lost.'

Bella gritted her teeth. 'Everyone lets you win because you're the Sheikh—*ob*viously.'

'You think so?'

'If you're not afraid to be beaten, then you'd let me race you.'

'What would be the point? You cannot possibly win such a race, *habibiti*.'

Bella put her hands on her hips, her irritation increasing by the minute. 'Watch me! Watch me as I disappear into the distance, Your Highness. You can't possibly swim that fast because you're hauling the weight of your ego—'

He was still laughing, as if the mere thought of being beaten had genuinely entertained him. 'You are the most aggravating female I've ever met. And you really do need to learn to show respect.'

'Respect should be earned.'

'I agree. So when I win, this ends.' His smile faded and his tone was suddenly hard. 'You will stop annoying me on purpose in the hope that I will return you to the city. I am prepared to give you a start.'

As infuriated by his patronising tone as she was by his arrogance, Bella faced him. 'I don't need any favours.' Holding his gaze, she undid the belt she'd made for herself. Reluctant to spend another hour plaiting date-palm leaves, she flung it out of the water and watched as it landed with a splat in the sandy dust by the side of the pool. Then she grabbed the hem of her robe and stripped it over her head.

Get a load of that, handsome, she thought smugly and had the satisfaction of hearing the breath hiss through his teeth.

Without looking at him she bunched the robe into a ball and threw it nonchalantly after the belt. Standing only in her wet bra and pants, she turned and gave him a sunny smile.

'I was wearing more clothes than you. That gave you an unfair advantage,' she said airily, but her heart thudded as she saw the blaze of disapproval in his eyes and a tiny part of her wondered just what he'd do if she *did* push him too far. 'That's all the start I need. Ready, steady, go!' Without waiting for his response, Bella plunged forward into the water, lithe as an otter, driving forward in a stylish front crawl that was the result of endless races with her siblings in the lake at Balfour Manor.

At school she'd been unbeaten in the swimming races and she was confident that, over a short distance, she'd be the winner. She was fast, light and strong and she had the additional advantage that he clearly underestimated women. So confident was she of success that when she turned her head to breathe and saw him passing her, she felt a flash of shock. Shock was immediately eclipsed by a burning determination to win and Bella put her all into the last few strokes, her heart pounding and her lungs bursting with the effort.

He beat her by a full length and he wasn't even breathing hard.

Hauling air into her struggling lungs, Bella saw his amused smile and silently plotted all sorts of retribution.

'I offered you a start,' he said mildly, reaching forward and removing some weed from her hair. 'You should have taken it.'

Bella felt her vision darken and in the distance she heard him mutter something in a language she didn't understand. Then he was scooping her up in his arms and placing her gently by the side of the pool.

'Why did you push yourself so hard?' His tone rough, he sprang from the pool, water streaming from his body, his hair slick to his head. 'You are recovering from heatstroke. You should be taking it easy in the shade. You are the most aggravating, infuriating woman I've ever met.'

'And I love you too.' But Bella kept her head down for a moment, deeply humiliated that she was showing weakness yet again. *Macho man was going to love this.* 'If you're going to gloat, please go and do it from a distance. I just need a minute.'

'What you need is a lesson in humility.' He paused, his expression thoughtful as he studied her face. 'You're a surprisingly good swimmer.'

The dizziness cleared slightly. 'I'm a good swimmer *for a woman*, isn't that what you're saying? Savour your victory while you can—I'll beat you next time.'

'There won't be a next time.' His bronzed shoulders gleamed strong and powerful under the bright sunlight. 'Put some clothes on, Kate. And stop trying to provoke me. I won the race. You stay.'

Bella squeezed the water out of her hair. Every

part of her body was tingling with awareness and it was impossible not to stare at his strong legs and board-flat stomach.

His gaze lingered on her bra, which was now little more than a transparent film.

Bella had a sudden urge to cover herself, which was ridiculous because she'd never been prudish or self-conscious about her body. She was used to being photographed from every angle, accustomed to being studied by men.

But this man was different.

Ignoring the sizzle of awareness low in her belly, she stood gracefully, instinctively exploiting the advantage she had over him. 'Take me back to the city, Your Highness.'

She saw the sudden flare of anger in his eyes and then his hand closed around her wrist and he pulled her against him. 'You play a very dangerous game.' Pressed against his hard, damp body Bella felt an instant rush of chemistry. Exasperated by her response she twisted her wrist, but it was like being held in a vice.

'Let me go. I'm not your type and you're *certainly* not mine.'

His answer was to scoop her up in his arms and Bella gave a gasp of shock.

"Where do you think you're taking me? You

can't just throw me over your shoulder like a caveman,' she muttered, conscious of his hands on her
bare thighs and trying to ignore the tiny voice in
her head that said she didn't know another man
who could lift her with such ease.

He didn't pause in his stride. 'We're alone in
the desert, *habibiti*. I can do anything I please.
And I intend to.'

'What's that supposed to mean? You're proving
you're the Sheikh? I've got news for you, *Your
Highness*—I don't do as I'm told.'

'Then it's time you learned.' Tough and unyielding, he strode into the tent and deposited her on
the floor as if touching her had burned him.

'You can't just—'

With a warning growl he clasped her face in
his hands and brought his mouth down on hers
with raw, untamed hunger. As their lips collided
the chemistry exploded, the sudden eruption of
passion so primitive that it was like being caught
in white water. Bella was swept along, her senses
churning and tumbling, unable to escape the
flow of searing excitement that shot through her
body.

Her mouth opened under the demands of his
and she felt the erotic stroke of his tongue and
the pressure of his hand on her back as he pulled

her against him. As their bodies touched, Bella melted. Her head swam, her knees weakened and everywhere there was heat—around her, inside her, frying her nerve endings. With a moan of desperation, she wrapped her arms around his neck and kissed him back, fascinated by the strength of his shoulders and the sheer power of his masculine frame. But the biggest high came from knowing that he wanted her. He wanted *her*. Not Bella Balfour. It was the woman he was interested in, not the name or the family connections.

He made her feel beautiful, desirable—*irresistible*—and she gasped as she felt his hands on her breasts, his touch unerring as he removed her bra and dragged his thumbs over the swollen peaks.

He didn't speak and neither did she, but their actions said everything as they feasted on each other's mouths and savoured each fresh exploration. When his hand moved lower Bella closed her eyes, and when he finally touched her *there*, she shivered and buried her face in his neck, breathing in his masculine scent and savouring the roughness of his jaw with her tongue.

She was so lost in the fire he'd created that she didn't protest when he lifted her off her feet and lowered her gently onto the mattress. His muscles bunched as he supported her weight and then he drew back slightly, scanning her semi-naked form with eyes that glittered dark with raw, masculine desire.

'You are truly beautiful,' he said huskily, and then he removed the last of her flimsy protection with a single confident slide of his hand. Naked, Bella felt a flicker of uncertainty but he shifted his body so that he was covering her, the movement oddly protective. Mesmerised by the startling beauty of his eyes, Bella gazed up at him and then tensed as she felt the skilled slide of his fingers touching her intimately. It was maddeningly, impossibly good and she gave a moan of disbelief and tried to say something but his mouth covered hers again, silencing her incoherent whimper. Displaying an expertise far beyond anything she'd ever experienced before, he created a storm of pleasure so intense that she felt desperate. She'd never wanted anything or anyone as much as she wanted this man. Her pelvis was burning and she shifted frantically, trying to ease the almost agonising pressure, but he refused to release her from her sensual agony.

'Please,' she gasped, dragging her hand down his back in an attempt to urge him closer. 'Please... oh, please, can you just—'

His answer was to fasten his mouth over the tip of her breast and Bella moaned as another explosion of heat erupted inside her, the dark feverish pleasure almost too much to bear.

'Please...I really need—'

He muttered something in a driven tone, looked at her with eyes blazing dark with passion and then slid a strong hand under her bottom and shifted her beneath him in a purposeful movement that brought her into contact with the powerful thrust of his erection. He was dominant and decisive, very much the controlling male, but Bella didn't even care—all she cared about was that he do *something* about the desperate craving that was threatening to eat her alive.

'Now,' she begged frantically, and he positioned her the way he wanted her and surged into her quivering, throbbing flesh with a single smooth thrust that joined them completely.

He gave an earthy groan and dropped his head onto her shoulder, his breathing harsh and unsteady as he fought for control.

The feel of him inside her was so shockingly good that Bella couldn't breathe or move. As he surged into her again, she dug her nails into his flesh and arched against him, moving her hips in response to the urgent rhythm he'd set. It was frenzied, fast and frantic, and almost immediately she shot into a climax so ferociously intense that she couldn't catch her breath. Again and again he drove her to the same point and then finally, when her mind was blurred and she thought she might actually pass out, he muttered something against her mouth and gave a final thrust that sent them both slamming hard into a solid wall of sensation.

This time Bella was completely out of control, her body overwhelmed by such crazy levels of excitement that she clung to him and sobbed against his sleek skin. Even as the spasms gradually faded she didn't let go of him. She *couldn't* let go of him. She wanted to hold him forever. In the depths of her passion-soaked brain, she felt as though everything had changed but she couldn't identify what or why. All she knew was that they'd shared something incredible. She felt sexy, and cared for and *special*.

The light flooded the opening of the tent and the intense heat shimmered around them, as if the sun was smiling approval. Bella lifted her hand and touched his hair, noticing that it was almost blue-black in colour.

He must have felt her touch because he lifted his head and looked down at her. She noticed that his jaw was the same blue-black as his hair, that his lashes were long and thick and that he had beautiful cheekbones—and she saw that his deep dark eyes were blank of expression.

He was obviously as shell-shocked as she was, Bella thought weakly. Her hair was sticking to her neck; she felt wrung out by the heat and by the whole experience. In all the things that had gone wrong lately, this felt completely right. It was the single most thrilling moment of her life. And suddenly she was desperate for him to just hold her. That was all she wanted. A hug.

Tentatively she placed her hand on his chest, the tips of her fingers tingling as she encountered hard muscle and dark body hair. His body was incredible—all golden skin and tightly defined muscle. Glancing up at him, Bella suddenly realised that she felt shy for the first time in her life.

His eyes held hers and then he gave a brief nod of satisfaction. 'So you *are* capable of being submissive,' he drawled in a flat tone, and Bella blinked because whatever she'd been expecting him to say, it hadn't been that.

Her bubble of pleasure popped.

Shame slid over her. What had made her think, even for a moment, that they'd shared something special? Was she so desperate for affection that she had to magic it out of nothing?

Slowly she removed her hand from his chest, trying to control her breathing, trying to look casual and not to let him see how much his comment had hurt her.

So was that what this had been about to him? An exercise in male dominance?

She'd thought they'd shared something special and all the time he'd been putting her in her place. And she'd fallen for it, hadn't she? She'd gone along with the whole tough macho seduction routine without so much as a 'wait a minute.'

She'd been so desperate she'd begged him.

Bella blinked furiously. Suddenly she felt frighteningly empty, emptier than ever before. 'I'm not submissive.' It was a struggle to keep her voice light but she was determined she was going to do it. *Determined that he wasn't going to know.* 'Just lazy. I lay on my back. You had to do all the work.'

He stared down at her for a long, disturbing moment and then rolled away from her and sprang to his feet. Everything he did was confident. Sure. Catching her first proper glimpse of his naked body, Bella stared. Wide shoulders, golden skin, long strong legs. She gazed after him hungrily as he prowled to the far side of the tent.

Away from her.

Everyone always walked away from her.

He dressed without once looking in her direction. Which was a good thing, because it meant that she could remove a stray tear without him noticing. The lump in her throat was harder to shift.

The sudden urge to talk to her twin sister almost flattened her. That wasn't an option, was it? Not only had Olivia been banished to Australia, her sister wouldn't have *wanted* to talk to her. They hadn't spoken since the row. *Since that awful night.*

Bella watched him in numb silence. What had she expected? That she could fill that gap inside her with a moment of passion? Had she thought it would be something more? She was useless at relationships. All relationships.

Bella thought she wanted to be on her own and then she saw him finish dressing and realised that she really didn't.

'Where are you going?' She blurted out the question before she could stop herself and he lifted his head and looked at her. For a moment they just stared at each other and then he reached for his dagger and secured it in his belt.

There was something about the cold, hard set of his profile that made her stomach quake and suddenly her insides were a mass of insecurity.

'Did I do something wrong?' The moment the words left her lips she wanted to drag them back in, but it was too late and she cringed as she listened to herself.

Talk about needy.

Without answering, he strode towards the opening of the tent and Bella felt the tears burn her eyes.

'Don't you *dare* just walk out on me,' she flung at him, and he turned then—*this man with whom she'd shared the ultimate intimacy*—and gave her a look that froze her blood.

'That was—' he inhaled deeply '—a mistake.'

'Finally we agree on something.' Trying to keep her dignity, Bella reached for the thin sheet and covered herself. 'It was your fault.'

Something flared in his eyes. 'You could have refused me.'

'How? You weren't exactly taking no for an answer.'

His head jerked back as if she'd slapped him. 'If you'd said no, I would have stopped.'

Bella's face turned scarlet. Was she supposed to confess that she hadn't been able to think, let alone speak? Was she supposed to confess that she hadn't *wanted* to say no?

'You're the Sheikh,' she said flippantly. 'I didn't think I was allowed to say no to you.'

'Since when has that stopped you?' His mouth tightened. 'It will *not* happen again.'

Bella's ego crumbled into the dust. So much for feeling sexy and wanted. *So much for thinking they'd shared something special.*

'That's fine by me,' she snapped but she was talking to the thick, oppressive air in the tent because he'd walked out, leaving her alone.

CHAPTER FIVE

'I've never had a one-night stand, Amira.' Bella leant her forehead against the mare's sleek warm coat and rubbed her hand gently over her back. 'The newspapers print all those fictitious stories about me because it sells their papers and I play up to it, but if they knew how little experience I've had, they'd die of shock. I'm nothing like your master, who must have had quite a lot of experience if his virtuoso performance was anything to go by.'

The horse whickered softly, turned her head and nudged her gently.

'I can't take you for a ride,' Bella said humbly, warmed by the animal's response to her. 'Remember what happened last time? I almost killed you and I'm not risking that again. I don't care about me, but you're really special.' She kissed the horse and then tensed as she heard the sound of hooves from behind her. Wary, she turned and saw the Sheikh, and her tummy clenched.

Even on the horse, he looked spectacular—sleek, handsome and totally in control.

Reining in the stallion he sat still, looking at her, his hands steadying the powerful horse. Remembering how those hands had felt on her body, Bella felt an unwelcome rush of heat.

'Nice ride, Your Highness?' She'd pulled on her tunic again, but now she was regretting having cut it so short. For once, she wished she was covered up. Determined not to let him see how uncomfortable she felt, she made a fuss of the horse, aware that he was watching her.

'My name is Zafiq.'

'Ahh, and I get to use your name because we had sex, is that right? Special privileges.'

The breath hissed through his teeth and he vaulted from the horse and strolled across to her. 'You are very flippant.'

'Well, I'm sorry if I don't please you, but I have no idea what to say in this situation.' Self-conscious and angry, Bella pushed her hair away from her face, wishing she could have spent three hours being pampered in a spa before meeting him again. Facing him bare of make-up required a confidence she didn't possess. 'If this had happened in the city we wouldn't have had to see each other again.'

'This would never have happened in the city. In the city I don't forget who I am,' he gritted, 'nor do I forget my responsibilities.'

'Your life sounds like a laugh a minute.' Bella brushed sand from her tunic. 'I'm sorry I made you forget your responsibilities.'

There was a long protracted silence and then he sighed. 'Don't be. You were incredible.'

For a moment she thought she'd misheard him. She stared at a point somewhere in the centre of his chest and then slowly lifted her head to look at him, her mouth dry and her heart pounding. 'Sorry?'

'You have to understand that I am a very disciplined man,' he said fiercely. 'I am *not* accustomed to losing control.'

'Really? I'm hardly ever in control. I'm more of an impulse person.'

His smile was wry. '*That*, I have no trouble believing, *habibiti*. You're extremely emotional.'

'Whereas you are frighteningly unemotional.' Remembering how he hadn't touched her after sex, Bella felt her cheeks flush and turned away from him. 'So we're imperfectly matched, then. Having finally realised that, I suppose you've decided you're finally ready to take me back to the city.'

He inhaled deeply. 'That isn't what I have decided.'

'Look, this is supposed to be your week of rest and relaxation so you hardly want to be tiptoeing round an awkward situation, do you?'

'Precisely. This is my week of relaxation, therefore I shall spend it as I please.'

'What's that supposed to mean?' She rubbed her hand over the mare's neck. 'What pleases you?'

'*You* please me.'

Bella's stomach tumbled and she turned her head, her eyes wide. 'What did you say?'

'You please me greatly. You're extremely passionate and responsive and once you're in my bed you stop fighting me.' He gave a sardonic smile. 'Therefore I intend to keep you in my bed for the rest of my time in the desert.'

'So I'm going to be your personal harem while we're here, is that it?'

The corner of his mouth twitched. 'One woman does not constitute a harem, *habibiti*, although you certainly have enough spirit to share generously between at least ten women.'

'Now wait just a minute—' Flustered, her face burning, Bella backed into the horse who threw up her head and nudged her hard in the back, pushing her straight into Zafiq.

Strong hands closed around her arms, steadying her, and Bella moaned as she felt the immediate explosion of chemistry.

'You're not my type. I'm not your type. This goes against my better judgement.'

'Mine too—' his mouth hovered close to hers '—but I think we've suspended judgement at this point.' Without warning he swung her up into his arms and Bella thumped him on the shoulder.

'Where are you taking me?'

'Back to bed,' he drawled, striding into the tent. He deposited her gently on the mattress and yanked her tunic over her head without giving her the chance to resist. 'When you're underneath me you're soft, compliant and all woman so that's where you're staying while we're here.'

Bella gave an outraged squeak and made a grab for the tunic. 'That was a one-off performance, caused by too much sun and the fact that you bulldoze your way over everyone.'

He threw the robe out of reach, a dangerous gleam in his eyes as he stripped off his own clothes. '*Why* do you fight me?'

Averting her eyes from temptation, Bella glanced past him, trying to gauge her chances of making it out of the tent without him catching her. 'Once was a mistake—twice would be a disaster.'

'If you run, I'll just bring you back.'

She looked at him then and was trapped by his devastating smile and the unmistakable look of raw sexual intent in his eyes. Her body melted with a desire so intense that it was impossible to breathe. He was unreasonably, unfairly gorgeous. 'I'm not your prisoner.'

'No.' He retrieved the knife from the folds of the robe. 'You're an aggravating, feisty, defiant woman. And I find that unbelievably erotic.' There was an elemental primitive strength about him that made her shiver and Bella was suddenly acutely conscious that she'd never dealt with anyone like him before in her life.

Wary, Bella eyed the knife. 'What's that for? Are you planning to threaten me into submission?'

'Don't worry,' he purred softly. 'When I take you a second time, you won't be fighting me any more than you did the first time.'

Bella's heart was pounding and her mouth was dry. 'My brain is back in working order now. And this whole Neanderthal caveman routine doesn't really do anything for me. I like a man who can hold a conversation.'

'And I like a woman who knows when to remain silent.' He dropped the dagger onto the ground. 'I've watched you since the moment you arrived. And I was still watching you when you were writhing underneath me. It was a very satisfying sight.'

Squirming at being reminded of how easily she'd succumbed to him, Bella lifted her chin. 'That was all an act to protect your ego.' She tried to scramble to her feet but Zafiq gave a half-smile, caught her round the waist and dropped her back on the mattress.

'You are talking because you are nervous, and that is good because it shows that you are vulnerable. But you don't need to be afraid.' His expression thoughtful, he sat down next to her, every muscular curve of his bronzed torso so breathtakingly perfect that Bella found it almost impossibly distracting.

'I'm not afraid…I'm—' His mouth silenced the rest of her sentence and she felt her head swim, but she was determined not to make a sound. He already thought he was a god; there was no need to feed his ego by letting him know he was an exceptionally good kisser. Ignoring the rush of heat that swept through her body she pulled away and tried to look bored.

'Sorry, was I supposed to feel something?' But the husky note of her voice betrayed her and he gave a slow, masculine smile, closed his hands over her shoulders and pushed her back against the mattress.

'Are you ever honest about your feelings?'

No, Bella thought helplessly, thinking of the number of times she'd been hurt in her life. *Never*. 'I don't have feelings,' she whispered, and he lowered his head, his lips brushing against hers. Their eyes held, the connection between them pulsing, intimate and deliciously exciting.

The heat in the tent went from oppressive to stifling and Bella sucked in a breath as his thigh brushed against hers and his breath mingled with hers. 'Last time we took things too fast. This time will be different. This time we will drive each other crazy.' His burning gaze slid slowly down to her mouth, and then to her throat and finally to her breasts. Bella moaned as she felt her nipples harden against the flimsy fabric.

'*Stop* looking at me like that.' But her words lacked conviction because she didn't want him to stop looking at her. She *loved* the way he was looking at her.

Not as if she was Bella Balfour, party girl, but as if she was an incredibly desirable woman.

'If you didn't want me to look, you shouldn't have made yourself an object of interest,' he drawled, the deliberate movement of his hand sending another spasm of sensation arcing through her body.

Bella sucked in a breath. 'Take your hands off me.'

'Fine. No hands.' With a devastating smile, he lowered his head and drew her nipple into his mouth and Bella whimpered with disbelief as excitement flooded her pelvis in a heated rush.

'You really can't—'

'Yes, I can.' His voice husky, he covered her body with his in a decisive movement and took her face in one strong hand. 'Tell me no, and I stop. Is that what you want?'

Bella stared up at him helplessly. She felt trapped, feminine and deliciously aware of the hard press of his powerful body against hers.

Zafiq slid his hand down her bare thigh. 'If there's a no coming, make it soon, *habibiti*, because I'm a very hungry guy.'

Bella was hypnotised by the look in his eyes. She *ought* to say no. She really, *really* ought to say no. But right at that moment she didn't care that he wasn't suitable. She didn't care that they had nothing in common, *that this wasn't real.*

She wanted him so badly it was embarrassing.

Reading the desperation in her eyes he gave a slow smile of masculine satisfaction and her last coherent thought was that it was a good job the British tabloid press were never going to get hold of *this* story.

Zafiq brought his wide, sensual mouth down on hers with the assured confidence of a conqueror claiming the spoils.

Exactly as she had the first time, Bella went up in flames. He demanded everything from her, the erotic slide of his tongue stealing the last of her self-control. Her hands clutched at his shoulders, lingering on sleek bare skin, feeling the play of male muscle under her fingers.

He muttered something against her mouth and shifted slightly, his hand removing her bra with a single movement of his long fingers. Bella felt a sudden urge to cover herself and he must have sensed her sudden doubt because he shifted his body again, holding her pinned beneath him.

'You have a fabulous body,' he breathed, lowering his mouth and claiming the straining tip of one breast. 'A temptation for any man.'

Taking advantage of the fact he was distracted, Bella put her hands on his chest and pushed him onto his back. Then she straddled him, her blonde hair sliding over her shoulder and tickling his chest.

'Now we'll see who is in charge,' she said smugly, gasping suddenly as she realised where she was sitting.

He gave a slow smile of appreciation as he registered the same thing. 'Make no mistake, *habibiti*—' he groaned thickly '—you may be the one on top, but I am still the one in charge.'

'You think so?' Leaning forward, Bella trailed the tip of her tongue over his shoulder and felt his sudden tension. Smiling to herself, she continued to lick her way down his body until she heard him give a deep, earthy groan.

Relishing the shift in the balance of power, Bella drove him wild with her mouth and tongue, pinning his arms down with her hands and holding him there. Her prisoner. The delusion lasted all of a few minutes and then he flipped her onto her back with embarrassing ease and shifted above her, flattening her to the mattress with the weight of his body.

'You just have to be the one on top, don't you?' Bella gasped, her hair tangling with his arm as their bodies connected from shoulder to thigh. 'Has anyone ever told you that you have a power complex?'

'Has anyone ever told you that you're in-credible?'

The breath caught in her throat. 'No.' No one thought she was incredible.

Pushing that thought away, Bella slid her fingers into his silky hair and dragged his head down to hers. She wanted to forget, and if there was anyone who could make her forget, it was this man—and if there was a price to pay tomorrow, she'd pay it.

'So why do you keep a knife by the bed?'

'It isn't by the bed. It's by me. This is the desert, *habibiti*—' Zafiq turned to look at her and she saw that his eyes were actually a deep, dark brown rather than black '—there are always risks.'

And he was the biggest risk of all, Bella thought weakly, hardly recognising herself. This couldn't possibly be her, could it? Lying compliant and quiet next to a virile, dominant male. The desert must finally have affected her brain.

But this time she didn't make the mistake of trying to snuggle.

She couldn't face another rejection.

Just looking at him was enough to make her want him again and when he leant forward to deliver a lingering kiss to her mouth, her tummy tumbled and she waited in a fever of anticipation.

'Are you hungry?'

'Oh, yes,' Bella groaned and then realised that he was talking about food. 'I— Great. Yes. Food.'

He looked at her for a long moment and then pulled himself up on his elbow. 'This is *not* how I usually spend my time in the desert.'

Bella gave a faltering smile. 'Am I supposed to say sorry?' Suddenly he seemed remote and intimidating. 'Can you stop acting like a sheikh? You make me feel uneasy.'

'How do you want me to act?'

'Like a man.' Her eyes lingered on the dark stubble that shaded his jaw. 'You're off duty.'

'I'm never off duty. Responsibilities don't go away just because you are not looking at them.'

Unsettled by the topic of conversation, Bella gave a saucy smile. 'You've got to learn to relax and have fun. Talking of which—' She pounced on him, pushing him onto his back, using the element of surprise to her advantage. 'Now you're in my power.'

He looked at her with mocking, slumberous eyes. 'You think so, *habibiti*?'

'Surrender or be punished.' She nipped his jaw with her teeth, loving the rough texture—*helplessly, hopelessly attracted to his raw masculinity.* 'By the time I've finished with you, you won't need a harem.' *A girl could become addicted to his mouth.*

'You are a one-woman harem.' He groaned, cupping her face in his hands and bringing her mouth down to his with determined force. 'And you are driving me mad.'

'I have that effect on people,' Bella murmured against his mouth, her hair sliding around them like a gold curtain, locking them into their own private world. 'Just lie still while I drive you even madder.'

Zafiq poured milk into a cup and stared at the sunrise.

What was he doing?

An entire day and night had passed and the only time they'd left the tent was to cool down in the still waters of the oasis. How could he have lost track of time? *Since when had he had so little self-control that he couldn't resist a beautiful woman?*

He'd forgotten duty, responsibility—everything except the vivacious, feisty, incredibly sexy girl in his bed.

'Don't tell me—' her voice came from behind him '—you're standing there thinking we shouldn't be doing this.'

Zafiq turned and almost dropped the milk. Despite the lack of bathroom facilities her hair hung smooth and sleek over her shoulder, like honey poured from the jar. Her eyes were the same blue as the cloudless sky and they sparkled with life and happiness. He'd never met a woman so vital and energetic. 'For someone who can't wait to escape from the desert, you look remarkably content.'

'I *am* content.' Ignoring the cup of milk in his hand, she wound her arms around him, completely uninhibited. 'The desert is growing on me. I like some of its inhabitants.'

His senses overwhelmed by the scent of her hair and the warmth of her body, Zafiq stood stiffly, bemused by the feelings that besieged him. Accustomed to people treating him with the appropriate degree of deference and distance, he found her tactile, affectionate nature faintly disturbing. She had no idea how she was supposed to behave with him.

And he had no idea how to behave with her.

Struggling against his natural tendency to keep people at a distance, he finally lifted his hand to stroke her back but she'd already pulled away, her cheeks flushed and her eyes suddenly guarded, as if his lack of response had injured her.

'So—' her tone was a shade cooler than it had been a moment earlier '—what are we going to do today?'

What he wanted to do was drag her back against him but his years of ruthless self-discipline acted like chains, preventing him from freely expressing his emotions. He took refuge in the practical. 'You need to eat—'

'Is this breakfast? I've lost track—' She gazed at the mug in his hand and her lips curved into a cheeky smile. 'What's that you're holding? Milksheikh?' Glancing at his face, she shrugged. 'Sorry. That's my last sheikh joke, I promise. And I'll behave. I know you want solitude so I'll just stay here for the rest of the day and you can go and do whatever it is you do when you're by yourself.'

Zafiq looked up at the position of the sun and gauged whether he still had time to ride before the sun grew too hot for the horses.

'We will eat and then ride together.' He had no

idea what made him make the suggestion but suddenly solitude seemed less appealing than having this gorgeous, spirited woman by his side when he rode.

'Do you only ever give orders?' Taking the milk from him, she knelt down on the rug with easy grace and helped herself to a date from the bowl he'd prepared. 'Mmm. I love these. They're completely different from the ones at home.'

'Are you a confident rider?'

She nibbled the rich, dark flesh of the date and licked her fingers. 'Is that a serious question?'

Blinded by a sudden vision of her straddling him, Zafiq tensed, shocked into silence by the sheer force of his response to her.

She looked at him expectantly. 'I won't fall off the horse if that's what's worrying you.' Her expression was slightly puzzled, as if she was trying to work out what he was thinking. 'I've ridden since I was a child.'

'Your last experience on the back of a horse wasn't a huge success.'

'The riding was fine—it was my sense of direction that was at fault.' Her fingers closed round another date. 'Well, the horse's sense of direction wasn't anything to write home about either, but I suppose that's not her fault. The desert looks the same in every direction.'

'On the contrary, it is a varied landscape if you keep your eyes open.'

'That's where I was going wrong...' Bella finished her milk and ate a piece of the bread he'd prepared. 'I collapsed unconscious and I haven't yet learned to do that with my eyes open. This food is absolutely delicious, thank you.'

Zafiq found it impossible to look away from her. Kneeling on the rug she was like some pagan goddess—lean and supple, fit and strong, her long limbs a warm honey gold under the hot desert sun. Even without access to a bathroom mirror and a bag full of cosmetics, she dazzled. And she was a woman who knew how to use her looks. The fact that, right now, she was too busy gorging on dates and licking her fingers to worry about seduction made her all the more seductive.

Zafiq felt the heat streak through his body. *And he'd ordered her to spend the day with him.* Was he mad? 'The trousers you were wearing yesterday are dry now. Put them on. It will be more comfortable and protect your legs.' *And his sanity.* 'And stay in my tracks.'

'What happens if I don't?'

'Amira goes into deep sand and breaks a leg,'

Zafiq said bluntly and saw horror cross her features.

'Right. I'll follow you, then.'

'So you will behave for the horse, but not for me?' He was once again forced to rethink his initial assessment of her as selfish and shallow. Whether she realised it or not, she was constantly revealing glimpses of the soft, caring woman under the defiant, independent exterior.

'I've always been better with horses than people. I find them more straightforward.'

Zafiq paused with his hand on the stallion's head, wondering what she meant by that remark. Curious, he turned to look at her but she was making a fuss of the horse, her profile revealing nothing. She looked young. Vulnerable.

Reminding himself that there was no room in his life for a woman like her, Zafiq turned back to his horse. 'You need to change your clothes.'

He heard the soft tread of her footsteps as she walked away, but she was back only moments later, dressed in the cotton trousers she'd been wearing when he'd rescued her, her long hair now falling in a thick plait between her shoulder blades, secured by another strand taken from a date palm. For ingenuity, he couldn't fault her.

'Wear a scarf over your mouth and nose.' Hand-ing her a length of soft cloth, he showed her how to wind it around her face so that it protected her from the sand.

Just when he was confident he had his reactions firmly under control, she lowered her eyelashes seductively. 'Do I look mysterious? Is this where I do the dance of the seven scarves?'

Heat ripped through him, sharp and dangerous as a blade. Gritting his teeth, Zafiq secured the fabric and stepped back from her. 'You are obsessed with harems and dancing.' But the scarf simply accentuated her beautiful eyes and he caught her by the waist, virtually flung her onto the back of the mare, before turning away abruptly.

Never before had he struggled to stay in control. He'd taken it as an indication of his own strength but now he realised that his control had never been truly tested. Until now.

Vaulting onto his stallion, Zafiq gathered up the reins and turned to look at her. She sat easily on the horse, as lean and athletic as she'd been in the pool. And she watched him with those dangerously beautiful eyes.

'So what are we going to do?'

'I'm going to show you that there's a world beyond your laptop and your iPod.' His eyes clashed with hers and for a disturbing moment the future loomed in the background, a stark reminder that this wasn't his life. Or hers. Just an interlude. And then he reminded himself that the future had no place in what they shared. This was about the moment. This was about now. 'I'm going to show you the desert.'

CHAPTER SIX

BELLA urged Amira faster, screwing up her eyes as the horse's hooves pounded the sand into a golden mist. Ahead of her, the Sheikh's powerful stallion thundered across the desert and she gave a shout of laughter because each time she did this it gave her the most incredible high.

It felt fantastic to be back on a horse, and riding in the desert was the most exciting, exhilarating experience to be had.

She'd ridden out with Zafiq every morning and evening for the past three days and she couldn't remember ever being so happy. When they weren't riding they were making love or cooling off in the still waters of the beautiful pool or nibbling dates and talking.

She'd never felt so free.

Leaning forward against the mare's neck Bella shifted her weight and drove the animal forward, closing the distance. Over the past few days she'd watched and learned. No deep sand here, she thought, anxious not to harm the horse in any way, remembering everything Zafiq had taught her. The horse was fast, so fast that the scrap of silk protecting her face unravelled itself as she drew alongside the Sheikh's stallion. Thrilled that she'd matched his speed for the first time, Bella challenged him with a smile and saw his mouth tighten in disapproval and exasperation.

You're going to pay the price for that one, Bella, she thought to herself and then his eyes gleamed and he pulled away from her, squeezing every last drop of energy from the horse with his skilled riding. The black stallion seemed to float across the sand, his tail high, his neck arched— strength and power visible in every muscle of his sleek body. Watching the power unleashed, Bella thought to herself that horse and rider were well matched.

Finally Zafiq urged the powerful beast round the base of a sand dune and Bella followed, coughing as sand flew into her mouth.

She was still choking when a bottle of water was pushed into her hand.

'Drink.'

Bella drank, the water soothing her dusty throat. 'My scarf slipped. I've been swallowing sand for the past five minutes.' Despite the lateness of the day, the sun was still a fiery ball in the cloudless sky, the intense heat shimmering over the surface of the sand.

But she was protected now—hat, cream and the knowledge that the cool waters of the oasis waited for them back at the desert camp.

Glancing at him, she saw that his eyes were fixed on the horizon. 'You love it here, don't you?'

For a moment he didn't answer, and then he looked at her. 'It is the one place I can be myself without answering to anyone.'

'I thought you were the one giving the orders. Can't you just tell them to leave you alone?' The moment the words left her mouth she was embarrassed by her flippant response. Squirming on the back of her horse, Bella shrugged apologetically. 'I mean, you are the Sheikh. You make the rules.'

'My responsibility is to my people, and also to my family.'

Family. Responsibility.

Bella wiped her brow with the back of her hand, uncomfortably aware that the feelings inside her had nothing to do with the heat. 'But you have to think of yourself too.'

'That is why I allow myself five days in the desert.'

'Five days.' Bella took another sip of water, ignoring the lurch in her stomach. *One more day to go.* 'Wow. As holiday entitlements go, that's pretty stingy. You ought to have a word with human resources and renegotiate your working conditions. And why are you responsible for your family? Can't they look after themselves?'

'Our parents died when they were young. My brothers and sisters rely on me.'

'Everyone seems to rely on you. So if you like family so much, why haven't you married?' Bella handed the water back to him, distracted by the shadow of stubble that darkened his strong jaw. 'Don't you want kids of your own?'

'My wishes are secondary to the needs of my people. If it were my personal choice, I would never marry.' Zafiq sat relaxed on the stallion, his expression unreadable as he studied the wind patterns in the sand. 'But at some point I will take a wife, yes. And we will have children. It is necessary.'

'Wow. With that much enthusiasm behind it, how can it fail?' Bella felt a stab of emotion she didn't recognise. 'So when the pressure gets too much, you're going to pick a suitable wife. Someone with the right breeding.' Someone completely unlike her—*someone who didn't have bad Balfour blood and an uncertain temperament.*

'Of course.'

'What if you don't love her?'

He frowned. 'Love isn't a requirement. I will make sure that I pick someone I can respect and admire. That will be enough.'

'And she'll marry you for the status. Not because she loves you but because of who you are.' Her thoughts shifting to the discovery she'd made the night of the Balfour Ball, Bella couldn't keep the bitterness out of her tone. 'And what about your kids? How do you think your children will feel about that when they grow up? Do you think it's good for a child to know that her father never loved her mother? And what about your wife? Aren't you afraid she might fall in love and have an affair?'

'My wife would never have any reason to stray.' He spoke with utter conviction, his hand steady on the bridle as he watched her curiously. 'Are you going to tell me why this subject upsets you so deeply?'

'It doesn't upset me,' Bella snapped, and Amira gave a nervous whinny and sidestepped into Zafiq's stallion. With a show of superb horsemanship and controlled strength, Zafiq calmed both animals and Bella stroked a shaking hand down her horse's mane, horrified by her loss of control. 'Sorry,' she muttered. 'None of my business. Let's ride, shall we?'

'You seem to have strong views on marriage.' His tone was a shade cooler. 'Have you been married?'

'No! That's one mistake I haven't made.' *Probably the only one*, Bella thought bleakly, turning the mare and urging her back towards their desert camp. Why, oh, why hadn't she kept her mouth shut? The last thing she wanted to do was think about the mess she'd left behind at home.

Ironic, she thought to herself, that four days ago she couldn't wait to get back to civilisation. Now, she was dreading it.

Zafiq was by her side, holding the stallion firmly, refusing to allow him to surge ahead. 'You've never been married, and yet you have had men.'

'No, I was a virgin until I met you,' she said flippantly, wondering why she should care that his face darkened with masculine disapproval.

Since when had she needed anyone's approval?
She'd grown up disappointing everyone.
She should be used to it by now.
Horrified by the sudden weakness that had her

tempted to confess her whole messy life history, Bella urged Amira forward.

What was the matter with her? Why would she want to spill her guts to this guy who wouldn't understand anything about her life? And anyway, she didn't want to think about being Bella Balfour. She didn't want the name Balfour intruding on their few days of desert bliss.

Bella was so shocked by that thought, she pulled the mare to a halt again.

Bliss?

She looked around her as if she were seeing the desert for the first time. She studied the strange swirling patterns on the red-gold sand, the steep rise of the dunes and the sheer magnitude of the scenery around her. She thought of the sunsets she'd seen—of the blazing red ball of fire sinking down below the horizon and the incredible stars, shining in the night sky like diamonds against dark velvet in a jeweller's window.

'Now what's wrong?' Zafiq was by her side, his expression concerned. 'Are you hurt? Is the sand bothering you?'

Yes, the sand was bothering her, but not in the way she'd expected.

'I—it's beautiful,' Bella said huskily. 'We could be the only two people on earth.'

'A few days ago that would have horrified you, along with the absence of conditioner and a mirror.'

'I know. Worrying, isn't it?' Bella gave a humourless laugh and swiped a strand of hair out of her eyes. 'Now I *know* I need a therapist.'

'Time for reflection in the desert is as good as a therapist. Are you going to tell me what's troubling you?'

She didn't dare admit it was the thought of going back to civilisation. 'Do you ever wish life could just stay this simple,' she blurted out and saw his eyes narrow.

'I don't allow myself to think like that because I know it's not an option.'

'Don't you ever think about yourself?'

'Yes.' His gaze held hers. 'This week, I have pleased no one but myself.'

'You've pleased *me*,' she whispered, and Zafiq hesitated and then reached across and took her hand.

'Tell me what is wrong.'

It was the first time he'd touched her in a way that wasn't sexual and the moment was all the more poignant because she knew the only reason he was offering her comfort was because he didn't know her. Not really. Once he discovered she was

Bella Balfour—*once he heard all the scandal and gossip*—he'd walk away without looking back.

She removed her hand from his. 'What could possibly be troubling me?'

'You have told me very little of your real life.'

Because it was an empty, useless life. A life that mattered to no one…

'I'm here to get away from my real life, like you.' Bella stroked the mare gently and the horse snorted and stamped at the sand, sensing her rider's tension.

'You said your father sent you here—'

'Wasn't that kind of him?' She treated him to the dazzling smile she always used when she wanted men to lose the thread of a conversation, but he shot her a warning glance.

'Unless you wish to end up flat on your back in the sand, do not play your tricks on me.'

'I'm not playing tricks,' Bella lied, piqued that she was still unable to penetrate that iron control of his. Even though he was flatteringly attentive when they were in bed, she didn't fool herself that she was able to manipulate him. 'My father sent me here because he thought I needed a break. Tell me why the horses don't seem to mind the heat and the dust.'

Apart from a lingering look, he accepted the

change of subject without argument. 'The Arabian horse was bred to cope with the demands of this environment. The Bedouins were the Arab horse's first protectors.'

'So Batal has a good bloodline.'

'As does your mare.' Zafiq glanced across at her. 'To the Bedouin, yours would be the more valuable animal. They preferred mares. They rode on horseback to attack neighbouring tribes and steal their cattle, and a stallion would be more likely to make a noise and alert the enemy.'

'Girl power,' Bella said with delight, stroking the mare's neck. 'I had no idea Amira is so valuable. No wonder you were so angry when you saw me riding her in the desert. Sorry.'

'Don't be sorry. I may even have reason to thank you for your impulsive actions that day. The security at the stables was lax.' His eyes darkened like a menacing storm cloud. 'And I have my suspicions as to why…'

Bella looked at him expectantly. 'Well? You can't say something like that and then not finish the sentence! Why was security lax? To be honest I thought it was weird—one minute there were guards, and the next there was no one there. The place was empty.'

His jaw tightened. 'Amira is the most valuable animal I own.'

'If she's that valuable, why was she stuck in stables in the middle of nowhere?'

'Precisely *because* she is that valuable.' He hesitated, as if he were making up his mind whether she could be trusted or not. 'Breeding and racing Arab horses is a passion of mine. A lucrative passion. Unfortunately, some are jealous of the success I've been enjoying. The Al-Rafid Cup approaches and tensions are running high.'

'I presume the Al-Rafid Cup is a horse race.'

'It is a world-famous desert race that will be run a month from now. The winner of that race achieves much international prestige.'

Bella was intrigued. 'And my Amira is going to run in that race?'

'No, Batal will run in the race. And he will win.'

'So what's that got to do with Amira?'

'The tradition is that the winner receives the best mare in the loser's stable. If I lose, they will choose Amira.'

Bella felt a flash of horror at the thought of this beautiful horse going to a nameless stranger. 'So what are you going to do about that?'

He gave a deadly smile. 'I don't intend to lose.

However, I suspect that someone out there is exploring more creative ways of obtaining Amira. She is one of the most coveted mares in the world. She has already produced three Derby winners.'

Bella bristled. 'Then you should have had security!'

'There *was* security—' Zafiq gave a humourless smile '—but clearly something went badly amiss. If you hadn't wandered in when you did…'

'You think they were about to steal her?' Faint with horror, Bella tightened her grip on the reins. 'Poor Amira. That's so shocking—I wish I'd met them!'

Zafiq inhaled sharply and shot her a horrified look. 'That would *not* have been good for you.'

'It wouldn't have been good for them if I'd known they were stealing a horse!'

'*You* were stealing a horse,' Zafiq pointed out drily, and Bella shrugged defensively.

'Actually, I wasn't. Not really. I was borrowing her. Short-term. That's completely different.'

'Your moral code seems a little confused.'

'Blame it on two weeks in the Retreat. It drove me to a life of crime.' Bella rubbed her hand down Amira's mane protectively. 'So you hid her out here in the desert so that she'd be safe. But someone found out. And they were going to steal her. But the simplest thing would be to make sure that Batal doesn't win the Al-Rafid Cup, wouldn't it? So basically, both horses are at risk.'

'It would seem so.' Zafiq's eyes hardened and his tone was cold.

Bella tightened her fingers on the reins and glanced over her shoulder even though she knew they were the only people for miles. 'If you know who this person is, can't you stop them? Arrest them or something?'

'Not without evidence, although I do have people working on that.'

'You could just pull him out of the race.'

'No. Batal deserves to win. He will win.' The stallion swished his tail, as if he were agreeing with that statement. But Bella was still worried.

'But if they're willing to resort to theft—if Amira's that clever and valuable—I shouldn't be riding her,' she said humbly, and Zafiq laughed.

'Do you think I would have let you if I had not been confident in your skills?' His eyes warmed slightly. 'You have an amazing bond with her. I saw that when I rescued you from the desert. She didn't leave you. And you ride well. You have a natural gift with horses.'

Ridiculously pleased by his praise, Bella gave a half-smile. 'You think so?'

'Yes. And you are less self-conscious when you are around the animals. You have stopped looking at your reflection in my dagger and worrying about your appearance.'

Had she?

Stunned by that observation, Bella frowned and realised that it was probably true.

And she knew why. He made her feel beautiful. For once, she didn't need a mirror because she didn't feel judged.

'Before I was sent off to boarding school, I never thought about how I looked.' It was something that hadn't occurred to her before. 'I just spent my whole life in the stables. With the horses.' And being forced to exist without them had been torture.

'You owned a horse as a child?'

Thinking of the stable full of horses at Balfour Manor, Bella flushed. 'Well, I…rode quite often, yes. But not lately—' *Lately she'd been too busy messing up her life.* 'As a child it was my hobby.' She hesitated, looking back on those days with a slightly sick feeling. 'Three-day eventing— I don't know if you have that here. Dressage, cross-country and showjumping.'

Should she have told him that much about herself? Bella stared at Amira's mane, wishing she'd kept her mouth shut but then she reassured herself that Zafiq didn't know anything about her past. He wasn't going to know she'd been selected for the junior eventing squad when she was sixteen. *He wasn't going to have seen the newspaper coverage about her blowing her big chance.*

'Eventing takes considerable all-round skill.' He looked at her with new respect. 'Here, our passion is flat racing. It is a tradition that goes back centuries.'

'On a racetrack?'

'We have a famous racetrack in Al-Rafid, but the Al-Rafid Cup is raced in the desert.'

'Isn't that tough on the horses?'

'It is a short race, run in the early morning when the air is cooler.'

'But if someone really is trying to steal Amira, how are you going to keep her safe?'

'She is safe here, with us.'

Us.

Bella wondered if he even realised what he'd said. Somehow over the past few days, they'd become a pair. A unit.

She concentrated again on the horse's mane, terrified by what she was feeling. This man wasn't right for her and this life wasn't real, so why was she suddenly wishing she could stay in the desert forever?

Shaken by the thought, she glanced at the black stallion, who was prancing along the sand sideways, desperate to be allowed another burst of speed. 'He's so beautiful I'm surprised no one has tried to steal him too.'

'Batal is infamous for his uncertain temper,' Zafiq said drily. 'No one who prefers their bones to be attached to one another, would steal this stallion.'

'I think he's a very genuine, gentle horse.'

'With you he does seem to be astonishingly well behaved.' Zafiq gave a faint smile. 'It's a compliment. Batal isn't renowned for his people skills. If he were human he would have been sent to anger-management classes long ago.'

'I think he's sulking because Amira almost beat him in the race.' Bella watched as the stallion's ears twitched. 'Are you afraid of being beaten by a woman, Batal? Just like your master. That's why I had to let him win in the pool. To protect his male ego.'

'My ego needs no protection,' Zafiq drawled, and Bella narrowed her eyes and shifted in her saddle.

'Race me again, then. No favours. The gloves are off.'

'You are incapable of racing fairly. I can guarantee that the moment I'm about to start, you will remove your top or smile at me.'

Bella laughed. 'Am I that bad?'

'You are the most maddening, infuriating and seductive woman I've ever met.'

Her stomach flipped. They weren't words of affection, but hearing that he found her seductive was better than nothing.

Flustered, she changed the subject again. 'So shouldn't we tell the stables that Amira is safe with you? They'll think she's been stolen.'

'They know she's with me.'

'How can they possibly know she's with you? Does she have a homing beacon or something? Satellite tracking device?'

'I used the phone.'

Bella frowned in confusion. 'But you told me you didn't have a phone!'

'No. I said I wouldn't contact anyone to have you taken to civilisation.' He delivered the facts in typically masculine style. 'Unfortunately my position makes it impossible for me to be truly out of contact. The phone is for emergencies.'

'Your horse was an emergency?'

'She is a valuable animal. If I hadn't contacted them there would have been a search party and many people would have been inconvenienced—' he hesitated '—also, they would have come looking for you. And that would have led them to me.'

'So people really don't know exactly where you are.'

'No, but they know they can contact me in a crisis.'

'Can't they handle it without you?'

'I hope so.' Cool and unconcerned, he guided the stallion to the right, reading the ground and avoiding potential dangers. 'My brother is in charge—'

'Don't tell me—he's always been jealous that you're the eldest,' Bella improvised wildly, 'and while you're away he's gathering together all his supporters so that he can overthrow you. Maybe he's the one who wants Batal to lose the race.'

Zafiq's eyes gleamed with amusement. 'My brother feels nothing but relief that the burden of responsibility is mine. He is a mild-mannered, overly sensitive, generous-spirited young man who lacks confidence. And he has charge of my stables.'

'Sensitive and lacking in confidence? And

he's related to you?' Bella rubbed her hand over Amira's neck, a smile on her face. 'You're obviously at different ends of the gene pool.'

'He is my father's son by his second wife.'

'Oh—' Her smile faded. 'I'd forgotten you had a wicked stepmother too.'

'You had a wicked stepmother?'

Bella thought of Tilly and Lillian and flushed. 'No,' she said quietly. 'Not wicked.' *But neither had loved her, had they?* Even her own father struggled to look at her. *And now she understood why.* Everything had been revealed on the night of the Balfour Ball. 'So he's your half-brother.'

Zafiq frowned, as if the term somehow offended him. 'I think of Rachid as my brother in every sense of the word.'

Bella's heart fluttered as she thought of what had happened the night of the ball. 'So, you don't think it matters that you have different biological parents?'

'We were brought up together. We were raised as brothers.'

It was a different situation, Bella told herself numbly. His family didn't involve lies and deceit. 'You were really fond of your stepmother, then.'

Zafiq's mouth tightened. 'Didn't you suggest that we drop this topic?'

She glanced at his profile, stunned by the sudden change in him. He was remote and intimidating, very much the ruling sheikh. Clearly things weren't as smooth in his family as she'd first thought.

'Sorry, I thought—'

'Enough talking. I agree with your earlier suggestion—let's ride.' Without waiting for her response, he urged the stallion into a gallop, and Bella's mare threw up her head in excitement.

'At a guess I'd say he wasn't that fond of his stepmother,' Bella muttered, letting Amira have her head. 'Which just goes to show that families have a lot to answer for.'

She rode into the camp just a few seconds behind him, the heat closing in on her and her mouth dry from the dust. Sliding off the mare, she patted her and took her across to the water.

Almost immediately she felt Zafiq behind her. His strong hands closed over her hips and he wrenched off her tunic and trousers, his mouth on her neck as he stripped her naked.

'I have been waiting to do this all evening. Watching you on the horse has been driving me mad.'

Bella gasped, liquid heat pouring through her body and pooling low in her pelvis. Her knees buckled and she felt a rush of embarrassment because she wanted him so badly and she knew she shouldn't. She turned in his arms and kissed him hungrily, her hands sliding over his bare torso, her mouth locked against the fierce demand of his. They fell to the ground, onto the rug that still held the remains of their earlier meal, not even bothering to make it the last few metres to the tent.

In the background Bella could hear the horses drinking and a faint splash as something fell and disturbed the stillness of the pool. Somehow the sounds of the open air were more evocative than any romantic music had ever been.

I'm never going to forget the desert, was her last coherent though before he sank into her in a single determined thrust that joined them completely.

She groaned his name and his hand cupped her face.

'Look at me,' he demanded huskily, and Bella stared up into his eyes and realised she'd never experienced intimacy before this moment. Never before had she stared into a man's eyes as he made love to her, never before had she felt what she was feeling now. *It was so real.*

And yet how could it be real when they both had to return to their real lives?

How could it be real when he didn't even know who she really was?

ZAFIQ stood with the satellite phone to his ear, listening to the panic in his younger brother's voice. After making a few soothing noises, he sorted out each problem one at a time, issuing instructions and commands with cool authority. Only once did he falter and that was when his brother asked if he could cut his trip short by a day and return home early.

Zafiq's hand tightened on the phone, the fact that he didn't *want* to cut it short saying a great deal about his current state of mind.

Weakness, he thought grimly, cutting the connection and staring at the white canvas of the tent. *The fact that he'd succumbed to her in the first place was a sign of weakness.*

'Who were you talking to?'

Her voice came from behind him and Zafiq felt a stab of guilt as he turned.

She was standing in the opening of the tent, watching him with a smile.

The fact that her smile made him want to strip off her tunic and flatten her to the bed reinforced the decision he'd made.

'My brother needed to speak to me urgently.' He knew he was going to hurt her and he was surprised by how badly he didn't want to do that.

'What about? Is something wrong?' She strolled across to him, her feet bare, the dampness of her hair telling him she'd been enjoying the pool while he'd been on the phone. She slid her arms around his waist and Zafiq felt his body respond with predictable force. Heat erupted through him and he closed his hands around her arms and lowered his head.

Staring into those gorgeous blue eyes, something hard and uncomfortable formed inside him.

Was this how it had been for his father?

With a rough curse he put her away from him, like an addict denying a fix.

'Zafiq? What's happening? Why are you looking at me like that?'

'You've achieved your wish.' Stunned by the need gnawing at him, Zafiq reached for his robe and drew it over his head, forcing himself to ignore the urge to tumble her back onto the bed. 'I'm taking you back to civilization, *habibiti*.'

Silence greeted his announcement and when she did speak there was a frantic note to her voice. 'What? When?'

'Right now.' *Before he gave in to the wild, ravenous craving that was threatening to snap his self-control.*

'But I thought we had another day.' There was panic in her voice and the hand that pushed her hair away from her face was shaking. 'It's just— you said you were here for five days.'

She'd been counting.

Zafiq picked up his knife, his knuckles white as he grasped the handle. 'I am needed at the palace.'

'But—'

'*I am needed!*' He didn't look at her and it shamed him to admit even to himself that her influence over him was so great that he didn't dare look her in the eye in case he gave in to temptation.

Life gave you difficult choices, he reminded himself grimly, and the important thing was to make the right ones. 'We'll return to the city before dark.'

'That soon? We could stay one more night and go in the morning—' Her voice faltered and Zafiq took a step backwards, battling a powerful urge to take her in his arms.

'I'll prepare the horses.' Determined that this was one test he was not going to fail, he forced himself to ignore her slumped shoulders and strode out of the tent.

CHAPTER SEVEN

THE horses walked through dusty streets, past a souk selling brightly coloured silks, spices and jewellery and finally through an arched gateway that took them within the palace walls.

From the moment they'd entered the magnificent desert city of Al-Rafid they had been accompanied by mounted guards and Bella felt a rush of nostalgia for the simple life they'd led by the oasis. Astride his prancing black stallion, Zafiq was unmistakable as a man of power and authority and Bella had never felt more removed from him than she did now.

It didn't help that he hadn't once glanced in her direction since they'd reached the city.

Consoling herself that she was at least still by his side, Bella stroked Amira, taking comfort from the warmth of the mare's shiny coat.

Zafiq rode into a beautiful courtyard dominated by a central fountain and swung out of the saddle. Reluctant to leave Amira, Bella stayed on the

mare but he turned to look at her, his dark gaze
unreadable.

'The Retreat have sent your things. Your pass-
port and travel documents are all intact. You have
your wish—you are back in civilisation. There
will be no charges for the theft of the horse. You
are free to go.'

Go? Bella felt her insides drop. He was sending
her away?

For a moment she thought she must have misunderstood him.

He couldn't possibly be saying it was over, could
he?

For the past four days they'd been as close as it
was possible for a man and a woman to be. They'd
shared everything.

Well, almost everything, she thought uncomfortably, thinking of all the things she hadn't told
him about herself.

But this couldn't be about that. He couldn't have
found out yet, could he?

And Bella admitted to herself that she was
dreading that moment.

For once she'd been able to live her life outside
the persona that the media had created for her.

And she'd never been happier.

Perhaps he didn't realise that she didn't *want* to

leave. After all, she'd gone on and on about hating the desert and wanting to get back to civilisation, hadn't she? Perhaps he didn't realise that she'd fallen in love with the desert—and him.

Bella froze with shock.

No. That couldn't be right. Not love. She didn't do love. Men fell in love with *her*. Men made fools of themselves over *her*. It didn't happen the other way round.

With a shiver of panic, she touched the mare's neck, feeling the animal quiver in response.

'Miss Balfour?'

Hearing her name, Bella turned automatically and saw an elderly man studying her. *He knew who she was.* Her eyes flickered nervously to Zafiq but he was surrounded by people and she suddenly realised that up until this point she'd had no real sense of just how important he was. In the desert he had seemed like a strong, powerful man. Here, he was a ruler.

For a moment her mind flickered back to the unsmiling, cold man who had rescued her and then she remembered how he'd laughed with her, how they'd held each other in passion.

Suddenly she was desperate for him to smile at her again—

'I am Kalif, His Royal Highness's chief adviser.

If you come with me, I can make the necessary arrangements.'

Still staring at Zafiq, Bella craned her neck to get a better view through the crowd, only half listening to the man. 'Necessary arrangements for what?'

'For your journey home.'

Arrangements to have her removed from the Sheikh's life like some diseased piece of flesh.

She wasn't a suitable woman for a sheikh to consort with in public.

Knowing that she was not being given a choice, Bella swung her leg over the horse and dismounted. 'Thank you.' Determined to maintain her dignity, she followed Kalif across the courtyard, struggling not to look back. It felt as though someone was pulling at her head and it was almost a relief when Kalif led her through a heavy door and into an ornate corridor.

'Your things were forwarded from the Retreat, Miss Balfour. I have them here.' He led her into a large airy room, dominated by an antique desk and large, colourful tapestries depicting desert scenes.

Bella stared at her designer suitcase, feeling as though it had come from a different life. A few days ago she would have been desperate to lay her hands on it, but now?

Wordlessly, she crossed the room and yanked the zip down. Inside was everything she'd been craving. There was her laptop, her phone, her iPod, a mirror, make-up—all the things she'd learned to live without.

She had everything. She stared at the contents blankly, realising that the only thing she wanted was Zafiq.

That feeling of being wanted. That feeling of being connected with someone.

Confronting the unpalatable fact that for him it had just been sexual, Bella gave a twisted smile. *When had men ever wanted anything else from her?*

Kalif cleared his throat. 'The owner of the Retreat asked me to deliver a message to you.'

Staring down at the stark reminder of her real life, Bella barely heard him. 'What was the message?'

'He said that he hopes you will find peace.'

'Fat chance,' Bella muttered, zipping the bag closed so violently that the mechanism jammed.

'Bella Balfour?'

Zafiq's hand whitened on the newspaper article.

Dropping it on his desk, he picked up the next one, this time a glossy gossip magazine with a stunningly beautiful blonde snapped arriving at Balfour Manor for the annual ball. The headline was *Bella of the Ball* and the girl was wearing a shocking dress so short that it barely skimmed the top of her incredible legs. Her blonde hair gleamed like a sunflower on a summer day and her bold blue eyes flirted with the camera.

She was so impossibly glamorous he barely recognised her as the girl who had plaited her hair and tied it with the leaf of a date palm. *The girl who had galloped across the sand, an expression of sheer happiness on her face.*

Kalif cleared his throat. 'As you can see, Your Highness, she is extremely high profile.'

Zafiq gave a hollow laugh as he flicked through the magazines.

Fashion icon.

Party queen.

He only needed to briefly scan what was in front of him to know that the woman he'd become obsessed with bore a striking similarity to his late stepmother.

With no qualm or conscience, Bella Balfour had flirted with him and slept with him. He couldn't even blame it on misunderstanding because she'd actually given him a false name.

None of the emotions she'd expressed had been genuine.

Shock held him rigid, the raw tension in his powerful frame the only outward manifestation of his inner pain.

For the first time ever, he'd let a woman close. And not any woman—*this* woman.

'The newspaper editors must have felt as though they've been operating in their own desert over the past few weeks without Bella Balfour to give them material.' Somehow he kept his voice level. 'There must have been a panic when she disappeared. It's fortunate I contacted the Retreat. I'm surprised her family didn't have a search party out looking for her.'

'It appears that Miss Balfour has a reputation for being involved in somewhat wild goings-on,' Kalif murmured, his expression neutral. 'Her disappearance caused nothing more than a few raised eyebrows.'

Digesting that piece of information, Zafiq stared sightlessly out of the window. *Wild goings-on.*

It was like listening to the complaints he'd heard about his stepmother.

'Where is Miss Balfour now?'

'I have had her taken to a bedroom suite, Your Highness. Given that there is no flight to England until tomorrow afternoon, it seemed like the best plan. Miss Balfour seemed rather subdued.'

'Subdued?' Zafiq gestured to the newspapers with a sweep of his hand. 'Are we talking about the same woman?'

Kalif hesitated. 'She looked pale after the ride through the desert. I took the precaution of asking the palace physician to examine her.'

Clearly she was worried that her lies had been exposed.

And the fact that she was still in his palace disturbed him more than he wanted to admit.

Somewhere, right now, she was probably standing naked under a shower, letting the water cool her beautiful body as she'd done so many times over the previous few days.

Picking up another newspaper, Zafiq stared at the headline in blank silence.

Balfour Family in Ruins.

'This woman appears to make the front pages with monotonous regularity. Clearly she is an inveterate attention seeker. Thank you, Kalif,' he said softly. 'Don't let me delay you. I know you have things to do.'

'Yes, Your Highness.'

As his chief adviser melted out of the room Zafiq stood without moving, his eyes fixed on the gorgeous, glamorous girl on the pages in front of him.

Was it any wonder he'd behaved like a sex-starved adolescent? He was a red-blooded male and Bella Balfour was a distractingly beautiful woman.

But it hadn't just been her beauty that had appealed to him—it had been her spirit, her vitality, *her lack of deference.*

There had been times when he could cheerfully have throttled her and other times when he'd relished the challenge she'd presented.

She'd excited him as no other woman ever had and she hadn't been afraid to stand up to him. Nor had she been afraid to lie.

Not once during the intimacy they'd shared had she told him who she really was.

And that, he thought grimly as he scooped all the papers up and deposited them in the bin, said everything that needed to be said about her. Bella Balfour was a wild child with no sense of responsibility or duty.

Holding that fact in his head, Zafiq swiftly showered, shaved and changed into a suit and tie, ready for his meeting.

Knowing she was there, in his palace, placed an almost intolerable burden on his self-control.

He wasn't going to go and see her, he told himself savagely, striding through the palace, oblivious to the anxious looks people were casting in his direction. Tomorrow she'd be back in her old life, and the temptation would be removed.

The one thing he did *not* need in his life was a wild child.

Bella sat at the ornate window seat, staring into space.

Her face was wet with tears and when she heard the door of her room opening she quickly turned her face towards the window, not wanting anyone to see her crying.

'I honestly don't need a doctor,' she muttered thickly, 'but thanks for the thought.'

'If you are told to see a doctor, then you'll see one,' Zafiq said coldly, and Bella tensed, anger shooting through her like the flame from a blow torch.

'Go away! I don't have anything to say to you. You're a complete and utter bastard, Zafiq.' She heard the door slam shut and wondered for a moment if he'd stormed out of the room, but then she heard his firm, confident tread as he walked towards her.

'I could have you imprisoned for that remark.'

'Is that how you dump women you don't want any more? You throw them in your *dungeon*?'

'I don't have dungeons,' he gritted, 'any more than I have a harem.'

'Careful, Zafiq, you're on the verge of losing that precious control of yours.' She pulled her knees up to her chest, not looking at him, devastated by his rejection. 'What are you doing here anyway?'

'I want to know why you lied to me.'

'I didn't lie. I just didn't tell you the truth.'

'*Stop* acting like a spoiled child,' he thundered, 'and answer my question!'

'Leave me alone.'

'Why are you sulking?'

'I'm not sulking. I'm thinking.'

'A whole new experience for you, I should imagine.' His acid tone stung and she gave a hollow laugh.

'Ahh…I see you've been reading about me. My life story in headlines.'

'Why did you tell me you were called Kate?'

'Because for five minutes of my life I didn't want to be Bella Balfour, OK?' Her voice rose.

'Try having a surname like mine and maybe you'd understand.' Overwhelmed by emotion, Bella turned her head and looked at him for the first time and immediately regretted it. He looked spectacular, his powerful shoulders emphasised by the cut of his expensive suit, his tie a bold splash of designer silk.

'Nice tie,' she said flatly, turning away quickly but not quite quickly enough. He'd seen the tears on her cheeks and he gave a soft curse and strode over to her.

'*Make* me understand,' he ordered in a thickened tone. 'I want to know what you were doing at the Retreat. I want to understand why you ran away and I want to understand why you lied to me.'

'It doesn't matter,' Bella said wearily. 'Why don't you just go and do whatever it is you do. It's over. I get the message. You don't need to hammer it home.' She heard him catch his breath.

'You are on the front page of every British newspaper,' he growled. 'You are *"Bad Bella."* You're the *"terrible twin."*'

Bella flinched—each ghastly headline felt as though he were throwing a brick at her. 'So why are you asking me? It should be quite obvious to a man of your intelligence why I didn't tell you who I was.'

'Why were you at the Retreat?'

She gave a hollow laugh. 'You obviously weren't concentrating when you read the newspapers.'

'There were rather a lot of them.'

'My father sent me away to think about my life.'

'A task at which you were clearly a spectacular failure.'

Feeling attacked, Bella drew her knees up to her chest. 'Absolutely. I'm pretty much a disaster at everything I touch. But that's what everyone expects and I hate to disappoint them.' Her flippant tone concealed oceans of agony and suddenly she was afraid she wasn't going to hold it together in front of him. She needed to drive him away. 'Look, this thing between us—it was just a fling. We both knew it wasn't anything else. You're not my type.'

'And you're *certainly* not mine.'

She gave a half-smile. 'Finally we agree on something. So let's just move on with our lives, Your Highness.'

There was a long, protracted silence. 'I expected to find you on your laptop. You were desperate to be taken back to civilisation. You used every trick up your sleeve to persuade me to bring you to Al-Rafid.'

At the beginning. Bella had to bite her lip to stop herself from reminding him that by the end she'd used every trick she knew to persuade him *not* to bring her back.

How did she tell him that she felt utterly defeated? *That nothing that had happened in her life so far had felt a fraction as painful as the fact that he was sending her away.*

'Look at me, Kate!' He muttered under his breath and jabbed his fingers through his hair. 'I mean, Bella.'

Something in his tone made her turn her head and, in that single painful look, they shared something so honest that the feeling drove the breath from her lungs. The seconds stretched into a minute and still the tension pulsated between them until Bella lost her grip on control.

'Zafiq—'

'No.' He snarled the word like an animal in pain and stepped away from her as if she were infectious. 'That is *not* possible.'

Bella felt as though someone had crushed her heart with a brick. 'Right. No. Of course it isn't. Silly me.' The pain in her throat was almost intolerable and she swallowed hard, trying to dispel the lump as he strode towards the door.

'There is a flight to England tomorrow afternoon. You're booked on it.'

Bella's heart dropped and she felt a sudden rush of panic. It suddenly dawned on her that he actually was sending her home. 'No!' For a moment she forgot to be cool or dismissive. She forgot to pretend she didn't care what was happening. She forgot everything except the fact that he was sending her back to England.

And suddenly she realised how calm and relaxed she'd felt in the desert with Zafiq. She'd discovered a side of herself she hadn't known existed. And now he was sending her back to her old life. There would be mirrors and bottles of conditioner, make-up and the whole of her wardrobe. Even without her allowance, she knew she could earn money. A single magazine shoot would make her enough money to survive for several months.

She'd be back to being Bad Bella Balfour.

And the paparazzi would hound her. It didn't matter what she did, everyone would think the worst of her because that's what they always did.

And the thought sickened her.

She didn't want to use her family name to make money.

She didn't want to use her family name at all.

'Whatever we shared is over.' Zafiq spoke with a brutal frankness that cut like the lash of a whip but Bella was past caring about pride and dignity.

'Don't send me back!' She jumped off the window seat and sprinted across to him, grabbing his arm with her fingers.

He shook her off, his eyes cold. 'We had sex, Bella. Nothing more. And don't pretend you're a stranger to that type of relationship.'

She didn't bother correcting him.

'You don't understand—' Her voice cracked and she cleared her throat and tried again. 'I—I'm begging you, Zafiq. Don't send me back.'

His gaze was hard and unsympathetic. 'What? No flirtation? Have you decided to go straight to feminine tears and bypass your usual seduction routine?'

'I don't blame you for thinking that way,' Bella whispered, 'but this is different. I'm not putting on an act. I—I can't go back. The press will destroy me, and my family has had enough bad publicity because of me. I just want to stay out of the way.'

'Then go and visit Europe.'

'I don't have the money—' Her face was scarlet and Zafiq made a contemptuous sound.

'So you *don't* care about your family. And you're asking me for money.'

'No!' Her voice rang with passion and her fingers shook as she rubbed the tears from her eyes. 'That isn't what I'm asking. I— Will you— I want you to give me a job.'

Stunned silence greeted her outburst and she didn't blame him. She was as shocked as he was.

'A *job*?' Zafiq looked at her with incredulous disbelief and then started to laugh. 'What sort of job? Chief troublemaker?'

His lack of belief in her stung, and she lifted her chin. Now he knew she was Bella Balfour he was making the same assumptions as everyone else. 'I wouldn't cause trouble—'

'Bella, you just have to walk into a room and trouble walks up and smacks you on the cheek,' he said wearily. 'And there is no job in my palace that would encompass your unique skill set.'

Suddenly she was determined to show him. *To show everyone.* 'You need someone in your stables,' Bella blurted out, catching his arm as he turned to leave. She felt the muscle flex under her fingers and removed her hand instantly, stung by the sudden physical connection that threatened to burn her alive. 'Please, just listen to me for a moment. I'm good with your horses, you said so yourself. Let me look after Amira. I'll be her groom. I'll train her. I'll sleep in her box. Anything, but let me stay here.'

'A job in my stables requires hard work and discipline. I have seen no evidence of either quality in you.'

'I can work hard!'

'When did you last get up at five in the morning and muck out a stable?'

'Never,' Bella said honestly, 'but—'

'Bella, you wouldn't last a day in my stables.'

Her eyes flashed. 'Give me the job and I'll prove you wrong.'

Zafiq stared at her in brooding silence and Bella swallowed, her heart pounding so hard she was sure he must be able to see it. This was a different man from the one she'd teased and laughed with in the desert. This man had never veered from duty and responsibility and she had no doubt that his authority was absolute. 'Please, Zafiq. Don't send me home.'

She saw indecision shadow his handsome face, saw his eyes flicker to her mouth, and then instantly move away as if the glance might have fatal consequences.

'My Master of Horse is called Yousif,' he said coldly. 'He has complete authority over the running of my stables. If he mentions to me once, just once, that you have been anything other than an asset, then you will be on the first flight out of Al-Rafid Airport.'

'Thank you,' Bella muttered, her legs melting with relief as she realised he'd actually agreed to her request. She told herself that it didn't matter that she'd probably never see him again—at least, not alone. The only thing that really mattered was that she didn't have to go home to her old life. 'Thank you.'

'You get one chance, Bella, and then you're out.'

It was back-breaking work.

Up at five every morning, Bella dragged herself down to the stables, so tired that it felt as though someone had attached lead weights to her limbs.

It didn't help that all the other grooms and trainers viewed her with nothing but suspicion.

Yousif, Zafiq's Master of Horse, was civil

enough to her but she knew he was waiting for her to slip up.

They were *all* waiting for her to slip up.

And she was concentrating so hard on not slipping up that she was like a cat on hot bricks.

But she'd promised Zafiq that she'd prove him wrong, and she was determined to do that, no matter how many nails she broke in the process.

She was allocated four horses to look after, including Amira and Batal, and she was horribly conscious of the responsibility she had caring for the Sheikh's favourite and most valuable horses.

But to her surprise, she loved the work. It reminded her of her childhood, when life had been so much less complicated.

She cleaned out stables, she groomed the horses but her real responsibility was Amira and she lavished the mare with love and attention.

'You're the only person who isn't waiting for me to slip on a banana skin,' she told the mare as she brushed the horse's coat, two weeks after she'd begged Zafiq for the job.

She wondered if anyone had mentioned to Zafiq that she was doing a good job.

Had he even asked after her progress?

'You are caring for Amira?'

Hearing an unfamiliar male voice behind her, Bella pushed her damp hair away from her eyes and turned, automatically braced to defend herself.

Had she made a mistake? Was there something she'd overlooked?

A young man stood watching her, admiration in his eyes.

Recognising the Sheikh's younger brother, Bella rubbed her hands over her trousers self-consciously, knowing she was filthy. 'Your Highness.'

'Do you know Amira has bred several Derby winners?' He strolled into the stable and stroked the horse's neck. 'Batal had better win the Al-Rafid Cup for us this year, or we will lose her, and Zafiq would be devastated.'

Bella felt her mouth dry. She wondered whether it was the mention of the Sheikh's name or the thought of losing Amira that made her feel so sick. 'Batal will win. He's the fastest horse I've ever seen.'

'Fast and difficult. He has just thrown Kamal, his jockey.'

'No!' Horrified, Bella dropped the brush she

was holding and Amira threw her head in the air, picking up the sudden tension. 'He fell? Why?'

'Batal spooked and threw him. Kamal has been taken to the hospital. He won't be riding in the Al-Rafid Cup.'

Horrified by that news, Bella curved her arms protectively around Amira. 'Is he seriously injured?'

'Broken bones. Not life threatening, but enough to make sure he can't ride Batal for the fore-seeable future.'

Bella thought of what that might mean for Amira. The black stallion was the only horse in the Sheikh's stables sure of winning the race. 'Someone else will have to ride Batal!'

'Batal is a killing machine,' Rachid said flatly. 'It is unlikely that any of the other jockeys will volunteer. Especially with Kamal now in hospital. He is the Sheikh's top jockey. If he can't stay on the animal, no one can.'

'The Sheikh has no trouble riding him.'

'Sheikh Zafiq is an exceptional rider. But he is not allowed to ride Batal in the race.'

Bella kissed Amira, unable to bear the thought of losing her.

What was Zafiq thinking at the moment, knowing that he was going to lose his favourite mare? She knew how much he loved Amira…

He must be devastated.

She tried not to think about the fact that two weeks had passed and he hadn't even come down to the stables to see how she was getting on. He'd visited sporadically, but always when she was off exercising one of the horses. And she was reduced to straining her ears to catch snippets of conversation that involved the Sheikh. And she heard nothing but praise. After two weeks of listening to gossip, it was obvious to her that Zafiq was universally adored.

It was also obvious that he was making sure that he didn't bump into her.

It was as if their relationship had never happened.

A mirage, Bella thought miserably. A fantasy conjured up out of the burning sands and desert heat.

She wondered if Zafiq's brother realised he probably wasn't supposed to be talking to her.

A terrible commotion came from the stallion's stall and Bella stopped thinking about Zafiq and hurried to the door with Prince Rachid right behind her.

'Batal is in a bad temper. He has only half killed

one rider today and he wants another victim.' He gave a humourless laugh. 'He reminds me of my brother. He has also been in a volatile mood since his return from the desert.'

'You probably shouldn't be telling me that,' Bella muttered, watching with a frown on her face as Batal kicked his box hard and squealed with fury. 'I'd better go and see if I can calm him down. What's the matter with him?'

'He needs to be ridden properly,' Yousif said wearily, hurrying across to the stallion who greeted him by flattening his ears to his head and showing the whites of his eyes. 'But His Highness is busy with state business, Kamal is in hospital and the horse will allow no one else on his back.'

Bella bit her lip. 'I'll ride him.' She put down the body brush she'd been using to groom Amira and wiped her shiny forehead with the hem of her T-shirt. Seeing Rachid's eyes widen she blushed hotly. 'Sorry. Look, you have belly dancers here, don't you? What's the difference?' Hoping her thoughtless action wasn't going to get her sacked, Bella hurried across to Yousif. After seeing the horrified reaction when she'd appeared in a pair of miniscule shorts on her first day, she'd been so careful to wear modest T-shirts and long trousers, reminding herself that it was better to boil to death in the desert heat than be sent back to England in disgrace. 'Let me take Batal onto the racetrack.'

'That is out of the question. It is too much of a risk.'

'For whom? Me or the stallion?'

'A girl of your little strength would be unable to handle such an animal,' Yousif said stiffly, 'and a woman riding alone would be inappropriate. Go to the main barn and order one of the other jockeys to come and ride him.'

Bella pushed her sweaty hair away from her face, tempted to stick her face in Batal's water bucket just to cool down. 'They won't want to. Not with Kamal lying in hospital as a horrible warning.'

'Go and tell Hassan. If he values his job, he will exercise the stallion.'

Bella opened her mouth to point out that Hassan probably valued his neck more than his job, and then closed it again. She couldn't afford to fall out with anyone. She was all too aware that her own job security hung by a thread.

Nodding to the grim-faced Yousif, she walked over to the barn and found several of the jockeys together, discussing who would ride Batal in the race that was looming closer.

'Hassan—' Bella picked out the jockey who had become a friend. 'Give me your clothes.'

The young man put his hands on his hips and grinned suggestively. 'You are seducing me, no? You find my masculinity overwhelming?'

Bella sighed. Had *everyone* read the newspaper coverage on her? 'No,' she said wearily, refraining from pointing out that after four days with the Sheikh, she had a whole new take on masculinity. 'I'm saving your job and your life. But I need a spare set of your clothes. Just do it, Hassan. I've been up since five, I'm hot and tired and my leg is sore because Amira just nipped me.'

'Lucky Amira.' One of the other jockeys offered her a bowl of dates and she helped herself with a smile of thanks, never able to say no to that particular treat.

'Good job I'm doing all this exercise or I'd be the size of a palace. Hassan, go and hide somewhere for a couple of hours. The rest of you need to say you saw him riding Batal.'

'I wouldn't ride that monster if it cost me my job.' Hassan handed her a set of clothes, his expression curious. 'What are you going to do with these?'

'Ride "that monster" so it doesn't cost you your job.' Her tone flippant, Bella walked to the back of the barn. 'Turn your backs.' Quickly she stripped off her trousers and T-shirt and pulled on Hassan's riding clothes.

Then she twisted her blonde hair into a tight knot and secured it on top of her head, promising herself that tonight she was going to find time to wash it. Only when she was confident that not a single wisp of blonde hair was showing, did she pull on the racing helmet.

'You're riding the stallion? Are you mad?' Genuinely concerned, one of the jockeys hurried over to her. 'Bella, you can't do that. You're a woman.'

'Oh, please—' Bella shot him an impatient look and pushed her feet into a pair of riding boots. 'Being a woman hasn't stopped me getting up at the crack of dawn and slaving in these stables. I learned to ride before I could walk. And anyway, do *you* want to ride Batal?'

The jockey pulled a face. 'No. I have a wife and children.' His expression sheepish, he looked at the others and they all looked away.

'Precisely.' Bella fastened the helmet. 'But one of us has to do it or Hassan will lose his job. Batal lets me feed him and clean him out without biting me. Hopefully he'll let me climb on his back.'

Perhaps he'd remember her from the desert.

Perhaps he'd remember that, for a short moment in time, she'd had his master's approval.

Walking back across the barn, Bella removed the scarf that Hassan was wearing around his neck. 'No one is expecting me to ride, so they won't notice. I just need you to cause a distraction while I fetch Batal from the stable.'

Hassan grabbed her hand. 'Why are you doing this for me?'

'Because you covered for me when I messed up at the beginning,' Bella muttered, struggling to position the scarf effectively. 'It's because of you that Yousif didn't go to Sheikh Zafiq, and don't think I don't know it. Can you help me tie this stupid thing?'

The jockeys looked uneasy. 'A woman shouldn't be riding alone…'

'You're forgetting—I'm not riding as a woman. I'm riding as Hassan. And anyway, I'm only taking Batal to do some track work. I'm not riding through the streets.' Bella fastened the scarf across her face by herself. 'How do I look?'

The men looked at each other.

'You have breasts,' Hassan muttered, his face scarlet, and Bella frowned.

'Oh. I'd forgotten about that. That's inconvenient.'

'Wear this—' One of the other jockeys gave her a silk jacket. 'It's the Sheikh's colours. Anyone seeing you will know you're riding for him and it covers your—' He cleared his throat awkwardly. 'It shouldn't draw attention and it might keep people away from you. Are you sure you want to do this?'

Bella thought about Amira. And then she thought how Zafiq would feel if he lost the mare he'd bred from a foal.

'Absolutely.' She helped herself to one more date for courage. 'Go and distract Yousif and leave the rest to me.'

CHAPTER EIGHT

ZAFIQ tapped his fingers on the table, only half listening to the interminable discussion on oil prices and investment strategy. Never before had his responsibilities seemed more arduous or his palace more stifling.

Glancing idly out of the window he could see the racetrack he'd had built a few years before. Close to his stables, it offered a training facility as well as a world-class venue for international race meetings.

A lone horse and rider galloped over the turf and Zafiq's eyes narrowed as he instantly recognised his stallion, Batal.

Batal, who had put Kamal in hospital two weeks earlier.

Having visited the young man daily, Zafiq had given Yousif strict instructions that no one but him should ride the horse.

He was resigned to the fact that the race was lost.

And if the race was lost, so was his beloved Amira.

But someone—he couldn't see who—was training Batal.

Whoever it was rode well, coaxing an impressive performance from the normally fractious stallion, keeping that leashed power under control with a light hand.

'That is Hassan.' His brother Rachid followed his gaze. 'He has been exercising Batal since Kamal's fall.'

'I gave instructions that no one was to ride him but me.'

'You've been incredibly busy. You had good reason not to spend time in the stable.'

Knowing that his reason for not being in the stables had golden hair and long legs, Zafiq felt the dull ache of tension spread across his shoulders. The sweet pull of temptation had been a constant companion since his return from the desert. It ate away at him, challenging his self-control.

'Hassan is to be praised,' he said in a neutral tone. 'I hadn't realised he possessed such superior riding skills. Perhaps the race is not lost after all.'

'He has surprised us all.' Rachid frowned. 'I wouldn't have thought it. I have seen him ride many times and he is competent, but not exceptional.'

Zafiq rose to his feet, intrigued by the sudden change in Rachid. Over the past few weeks his brother seemed to have grown in confidence, contributing to affairs of state in a way that he never had before.

Zafiq wondered idly what had caused the change.

Had being left in charge for a short time given him the confidence he'd lacked?

'Batal has been acting up all week, kicking out his box and misbehaving—' Rachid strolled to the window and watched the horse gallop around the track '—generally suffering from an excess of testosterone.'

All too familiar with the adverse effects of an excess of testosterone, Zafiq gave a grim smile and wondered whether a ride would relieve the almost unbearable tension.

Deciding that anything would be better than remaining in the palace for another day, he concluded the meeting.

He felt trapped. Stifled. The palace felt like a prison, his responsibilities like chains around his body.

'Is everything all right, Zafiq?' Rachid lingered behind after the others had left the room. 'You seem distracted. Are you worrying about the race?'

'Everything is fine.' This was his life. This was his duty. And he realised that he'd been neglecting his responsibility towards his younger brothers and sisters. 'I have not seen much of Sahra since I returned from the desert. She eats dinner in the fastest time possible and I've received no complaints about her behaviour for several weeks. Should I be worried?'

'She has been making a huge effort not to upset you.'

That revelation turned Zafiq's internal radar to full alert. 'Why? What does she want?'

Rachid grinned. 'You know women so well.'

'Sadly, yes.' Accustomed to his young half-sister's tricks, Zafiq braced himself for a shopping list. 'What is it this time? Diamonds? Dresses? Break it to me gently.' Turning back to the table, he started to sign the papers that Kalif had left for his attention. 'She is progressing well in her training to bleed some poor man dry?'

'Not all women are like my mother,' Rachid said quietly, and Zafiq felt an immediate spurt of regret that he'd allowed his feelings to show.

He put his pen down instantly. 'My apologies, Rachid.'

'You don't have to apologise. I made the comment, not you. And you don't need to protect me any more. I'm a man now, Zafiq, and part of being a man is facing the truth. You taught me that.' Rachid straightened his shoulders. 'I loved my mother, but that love did not blind me to her faults. I see now what trouble she caused with her extravagant nature. The fact that our people still support our family is because of their love for *you*.'

Stunned, Zafiq found himself struggling for the right thing to say. 'Rachid—'

'I know that my mother is the reason you are not yet married. I know you feel our father gave in to her, but Sahra will not be like my mother,' Rachid said firmly. 'She *does* want something, but not jewels or dresses. If you take time to talk to her, I think you'll find she's changed.'

Changed?

Everyone around him appeared to be changing and he hadn't noticed.

Cautious now, Zafiq gave up signing documents. 'If there is something she wants, why doesn't she ask me herself?'

'Because she thinks you will say no.'

Was he such an ogre? 'What is it she wants?'

'Her own horse.'

'A *horse*?' Zafiq couldn't have been more surprised if Rachid had told him his sister had wanted his permission to ride naked through the souk. 'Sahra is terrified of horses. I have tried repeatedly to encourage her to ride. I've hired instructor after instructor and not one of them has managed to persuade her to stay on the animal for more than two minutes. She hates it.'

'She has been riding every day for the past few weeks. She has conquered her nerves.'

Genuinely astonished, Zafiq spread his hands in question. 'So who is responsible for this transformation? Presumably Yousif has appointed a good-looking jockey that I don't know about.'

'Bella,' Rachid said simply, his eyes softening. 'She has spent so much time with Sahra, teaching her. And she's so brave and beautiful—she has been an inspiration to my sister. Sahra wants to ride like her, and—'

'Bella? Bella Balfour?' Aggravated that the mere sound of her name had the ability to ignite a firestorm within his body, Zafiq gave a low growl of impatience. 'So she has found a way to avoid working by spending her time with a princess. I should have guessed she'd do anything possible to avoid hard graft.'

'You're wrong. Bella works harder than anyone.

She helps Sahra when she finishes work. They've formed a bond.'

Zafiq's eyes narrowed because he'd never seen such strength in his younger brother before. 'What can Bella Balfour possibly teach Sahra that I would want her to learn?' His own discomfort made his tone chillier than he intended. 'How to use her looks to manipulate a man? How to ignore duty and responsibility?'

How to be exactly like his stepmother?

'She has shown great responsibility. No one looks after Amira and Batal but her. Do you know she even sleeps in Amira's stall now because she's so afraid someone is going to try and steal the mare? Yousif tried to persuade her to go back to her room, but she refuses.'

Zafiq ruthlessly dismissed an unwanted image of Bella curled up asleep in a mound of straw. 'Yousif should have told me he was having problems with her.'

'Yousif adores her. Bella has become a favourite with everyone, especially the stable lads. They all love her.'

Zafiq ground his teeth, perfectly able to visualise what skills had led to such a sudden burst of approval from the palace staff. He knew better than anyone how far she'd go to get her own way.

'Clearly Bella Balfour is more talented then even I gave her credit for.'

'Oh, she is,' Rachid said earnestly, missing the irony. 'She has made some training suggestions that have made a great deal of difference. And she is the only person Batal doesn't kick.'

Zafiq made a mental note to pay an early visit to the stable in order to watch Bella work her charm offensive. 'So where does Sahra fit into this?' His fingers closed on one of the sheets of paper and he scrunched it into a tight ball. 'Why has no one mentioned her friendship with Bella before now?'

'Because of the way you're reacting now! Mentioning Bella's name in front of you is a sure way of putting you in a filthy mood. It isn't like you. I've never seen you lose your cool before—' Rachid flushed slightly. 'I suppose it's because you spent time with her in the desert. That must have been a difficult situation for you.'

Zafiq, who considered himself inscrutable, was stunned to discover that he'd revealed so much. 'What do you mean, "difficult"?'

'It's obvious that the two of you didn't get on, but you're much too responsible a person to let her make her own way back through the desert so you were stuck with her. And I know she isn't your type,' his brother went on hastily. 'She's not exactly conventional, is she?'

Zafiq ground his teeth. 'Conventional? No. She certainly isn't conventional.'

'And rescuing Bella meant you lost your few days of solitude. We all know you would have rather been on your own—'

Absorbing his brother's interpretation of events in incredulous silence, Zafiq decided that it was better not to explore that particular topic in too much depth.

Rachid was still talking. 'Honestly, Zafiq, she has added a great deal to Batal's training. Before he threw Kamal she taught them something called a volte—it improves the horse's balance apparently. Bella thinks if we can calm him down, it will help him win the cup.'

'If we can find a rider who can stay in the saddle, then Batal will win the cup.' Striding towards the door, Zafiq felt the tension spread across his shoulders.

'Bella says it encourages engagement and power.'

'Bella says, Bella says…' Exasperated, Zafiq turned on his brother. 'What qualifies Bella Balfour to change the training regime of my horses?'

'She knows a lot about horses! Did you know she was selected for the British eventing team when she was sixteen?'

No, she hadn't mentioned that. 'Did she win a medal?'

'No, because there was a scandal and she ended up being deselected—'

'Now *that*,' Zafiq drawled, 'sounds like Bella.'

'You're so hard on her!' Rachid flew to her defence. 'She's had a difficult life—' He clamped his mouth shut as if he'd said something he shouldn't and Zafiq's mouth tightened.

'What do you know about her life?'

'Quite a lot. She's very chatty in the stables. Really down-to-earth and normal.'

And clever, Zafiq thought grimly. 'You're infatuated with her blonde hair and her blue eyes, Rachid. Don't let that blind you to who she really is.'

'Perhaps *you* are the one who is blind to who she really is.' Rachid spoke quietly. 'She's a really sweet, kind girl.'

Zafiq looked at him closely, suddenly questioning *why* Rachid appeared instantly more grown-up and mature. He'd gone from boy to man in the space of a few weeks. Reflecting on the possible explanation for a change within that time frame, Zafiq felt a chill spread through his body.

No.

'Just how far has your relationship with her gone?'

Rachid straightened his shoulders. 'That's none of your business.'

'Answer my question.'

'She isn't interested in me, but if she *were*—' Rachid broke off, and Zafiq made an impatient sound, engulfed by a tornado of emotions, none of which he cared to examine too closely.

'You could not find a less suitable woman than Bella Balfour if you searched the planet. She is bold, outspoken, fearless.' Catching Rachid's stunned expression Zafiq realised that he'd done nothing but list her qualities. 'And she's emotional,' he added swiftly. 'Dealing with Bella is like dealing with a child. She shows no restraint. She has no idea how to behave.'

'That's what I find so refreshing,' Rachid said earnestly. 'One of the drawbacks of our position is that people are afraid to be themselves around us. Don't you find that, Zafiq? Bella is always herself. She says what she thinks. She isn't afraid to challenge authority if she disagrees with something.'

Remembering all the ways she'd challenged his authority, Zafiq gave a low growl.

'Enough talk about Bella Balfour!'

It was time he paid a visit to the stables.

Her limbs aching from another long day, Bella collapsed in the straw that lined Amira's box.

The mare lowered her head and blew on her gently and Bella gave a groan and closed her eyes. 'I'm so tired I could die. It's riding that great brute Batal that finishes me off. He's all muscle and I'm so worried that someone is going to recognise me that I can't relax. Every time I ride him out, Hassan has to go and hide. It's completely *ridiculous* that I can't just ride as myself. I shall be glad when this stupid race is over. I'm only doing it for you, you know that, don't you?'

Clearly oblivious to the enormous sacrifice being made for her, Amira started to munch hay and Bella smiled sleepily.

'Ungrateful beast.'

She was drifting off when she heard the unmistakable crunch of a footstep in the yard outside.

Her senses on full alert, Bella sat up. Heart pounding, palms sweaty, she reached through the straw and closed her fingers around the heavy stick she'd buried there just in case.

They'd come for Amira.

Where were the guards that Zafiq had posted in the yard?

And then she remembered that the guards at the stables near the Retreat had been paid to be absent at the crucial moment.

Amira continued to eat and Bella stood slowly, holding her breath, careful to make no sound. She looked at the beautiful mare—*the horse that meant so much to the people of Al-Rafid*—and felt the full force of responsibility.

Once again she was all that stood between Amira and *them.*

Last time she hadn't known the risk she was taking. Now she knew, and she was horribly conscious that she was no match for a group of organised criminals.

Reminding herself that she had the element of surprise on her side, she told herself that she had to act quickly. No hesitation.

If someone was going to harm Zafiq's horse, they were going to have to go through her.

She watched, terrified, as a strong male hand grasped the bolt, shot it back and opened the stable door.

Her heart thundering, Bella grasped the stick

with both hands and lifted it, inching to one side so that she could hit the man and not the horse.

In the shadowy light she could see that he was tall and powerfully built and her stomach cramped because her chances of defending Amira against someone as muscular as this man were remote. Swiftly she revised her plan.

As he raised his hand to the horse Bella gave a hiss.

'Get away from her—slowly. I know exactly who you are and what you're doing and I have a weapon pointed straight at you. Step away slowly or I *will* shoot you.'

'If you know exactly who I am and what I'm doing, then why would you need a weapon? And it's hard to shoot someone with a stick.'

Recognising Zafiq's dry, sarcastic drawl, Bella's knees flooded with relief and she dropped the stick and sagged against the wall. 'Oh, it's you!' She pressed her hand to her chest, feeling her heart banging. 'You frightened the life out of me!'

'Is that why you were holding a stick?' He flashed a torch in her direction and Bella turned her head away, squinting against the light.

'I thought someone was after Amira.' She slid back down on the straw, wobbly as a newborn foal.

'What are you doing here? You wanted to give me a heart attack and finish me off altogether?' Now that her eyes had adjusted, she could just about make out his features and she wondered why she hadn't recognised him instantly when every contour of his body was indelibly printed into her brain.

'I heard a rumour that you were sleeping in the stable.'

'Why would that bother you?'

'Party-girl Bella Balfour living in a heap of straw, no hot or cold running water?'

'I lived in a tent with you for four days,' she snapped, her body still weak from reaction, 'and that wasn't exactly a five-star experience. Where are the guards?'

'Obviously they know better than to arrest the Sheikh.'

'I thought they might have been paid off, like last time.'

'The guards in Al-Rafid are fiercely loyal to me. They cannot be bribed. What is this about, Bella?' His tone was cold and hard. 'Rising at five every morning and working until your hands bleed? Sleeping with my horse? It seems you've gone out of your way to charm everyone, including my brother. What are you playing at?'

Taken aback by his savage tone and the injustice of what he was saying, Bella glared at him. 'I'm working, not playing. I'm working a fourteen-hour day and then I'm sleeping here. You think I'm having sex with everyone in your stables, is that what you're saying?' Still overwrought from thinking someone was going to steal Amira, her voice was shrill. 'You think that the only way anyone is ever going to have anything nice to say about me is if they've slept with me!'

He was across the stable before she could move, his hands lifting her in a single powerful movement, his body pressing hers against the wall. 'I want to know how far it's gone with my brother. Rachid is very young and he has no experience of women like you—'

Overtired, shocked to see him again and bitterly hurt by his cynical view of her, Bella exploded. 'I can't win, can I? I've been working myself to the bone to make sure no one could complain about me! I don't have a single decent nail left, I haven't washed my hair for a week and I'm covered in bruises from—' She was about to say *your stallion*, but just stopped herself in time. 'Frankly I wouldn't have the energy for sex even if the opportunity presented itself so you can take your jealousy elsewhere!'

'I'm *not* jealous.' His thickened tone cut through the tense atmosphere and his hands tightened on her shoulders. 'And your morals are your own business.'

'Then why are you so angry? If you don't care, why are you standing there yelling at me?'

'Because Rachid can't cope with a woman like you.'

'Rachid can cope with a great deal more than you think.' She thought back to the numerous conversations she'd had with the prince since that first day. 'He wants more responsibility, Zafiq, but the problem is you're so brilliant at everything he feels daunted! You need to praise him, make him feel good about himself! Not everyone is as confident as you are—being given responsibility helps confidence.'

'What do you know about responsibility?'

It was a fair comment, but Bella was too wound up to be reasonable. 'I know how it feels never to be given any! Your siblings aren't children any more. Take a tip from me—if you believe someone will always screw up, then they probably will. Why don't you try showing some faith in people and see what happens? You can practise on me for a start! I've been busting a gut here to make sure I don't put a foot wrong and you haven't once bothered to come down and say I'm doing well. You told me I'd last a day, and I've been here a month so stick that in your… your…Bedouin tea and drink it,' she finished lamely.

He released her so suddenly that she staggered and Bella rubbed her hands down her arms, not because he'd hurt her but because being held by him had felt unbelievably good after all these weeks without him. She'd been in a different sort of desert, she thought miserably. A barren wilderness without Zafiq.

'You seem to know a great deal about my family. You will tell me who has been gossiping about Rachid.'

'No one has been gossiping! I've talked to him in person. Believe it or not, we have quite a lot in common! I know what it's like to have a glamorous, high-spending mother. And I know how it feels to hear everyone around you criticising the person you were raised to love.'

Amira shifted in the box and Zafiq put out a hand to calm the animal. 'Our family situation is extremely complicated—'

'Don't talk to me about complicated!' Bella erupted, and suddenly all the emotions she'd been bottling up exploded to the surface, refusing to be contained. 'Six weeks ago I discovered that my younger sister—my sister who I've lived with all my life, my sister who I went to school with and played with—isn't my father's child and that my mother wasn't the saintly person I always thought she was. My father *hates* me, the whole world hates me, my younger sister hates me and even my twin has turned her back on me, so don't talk to me about complicated!'

Damn, damn, damn.

Why couldn't she be icily calm? Why couldn't she ever keep herself together when she needed to?

Her outburst was greeted by a prolonged silence and then he raked his fingers through his hair, his own control clearly challenged.

'You are *so* emotional. I am quite sure your father does not hate you,' Zafiq breathed, 'and perhaps it would be wise to consider the possibility that your sister has not turned her back on you, but been unable to get in touch. You've been marooned in the desert. And as for the world— the world's opinion doesn't matter.'

'Try seeing your face splashed over every newspaper before you say that.' Bella gave an undignified sniff and wiped her eyes on her T-shirt, furious with herself for crying. 'And maybe my father doesn't exactly hate me, but he certainly can't bear to look at me because I remind him of my mother, and that's pretty hurtful, I can tell you.'

'Your mother died when you were a baby.'

'Yeah—' Bella's voice was husky and she cleared her throat. 'All I had was a memory and that's not looking too good right now.'

'Your mother must have been an extremely beautiful woman and extreme beauty often brings complications,' Zafiq said quietly, and Bella flushed slightly, wishing she wasn't so aware of everything he said and did.

'Well, her beauty obviously didn't make her happy. And that's because she was stupid enough to marry a man she didn't love.'

'Like most women, you insist on linking marriage with romance.'

'With good reason!' Bella walked over to Amira and buried her face in the mare's neck, seeking comfort. She felt angry with her mother, angry with her father and angry with herself. 'My father thought she was in love with him, but she wasn't. She just wanted the Balfour name and the money. If you don't care about a person, you shouldn't get married.'

Her hand still on Amira's back, Bella turned to

look at him. 'It's inevitable, isn't it? If you marry someone you don't love, at some point you're going to meet someone you *do* love. You're going to meet someone who makes you feel something you didn't know it was possible to feel. And you're going to realise that feeling is more important to you than money or status. And it isn't going to matter that the relationship isn't possible or that you're totally unsuited—because once you realise you're in love, you've basically got two choices. You go for it, and you wreck loads of lives along the way, or you decide you're going to do the "right thing" and stay, making yourself and everyone around you miserable in the process because you know you've missed your one chance of happiness. So either way, getting married when you're not in love means you're going to wind up miserable.'

Zafiq said nothing and Bella turned back to the horse.

'The funny thing was—there wasn't any money.' Her voice was muffled against the mare's smooth coat. 'It had all gone and getting everything back became an obsession for my father. And my mother hated that obsession. She hated every-thing Balfour. So she had an affair. And she died giving birth to that child. My little sister, Zoe.

The one I messed up just before I came here.'
Crying now, Bella hugged Amira, past caring
that she was making a fool of herself. 'Do you
believe in justice, Zafiq? Is that why she died?'

'Are you crying for your mother or your sister?'
Strong hands prised her away from the horse.
'You are torturing yourself—' Without allowing
her to resist, he pulled her into his arms, hugging
her tightly, and it felt so good to be held that for
a moment Bella just stood there, breathing in his
masculine scent, revelling in the feeling of being
close to him again.

But it wasn't real, was it?

Until she'd started crying, he hadn't touched
her. It wasn't personal.

It was time she learned to stand on her own two
feet.

'Let me go, Zafiq,' she muttered. 'I know you
hate crying women. Sahra told me.'

'That is because Sahra uses tears like cur-
rency—she trades them for whatever she wants.'
Zafiq stroked her hair away from her face, forcing
her to look at him. 'Is this why you were in the
Retreat? Escaping from the scandal?'

It horrified her that he'd obviously read what
had been written about her. 'Which headline
did you like best? *Blue Blood Turns Bad? Ille-*

gitimate Daughter Revealed at Balfour Ball?'
The headlines were engraved in her brain and
she squirmed as she remembered the salacious,
vindictive things that had been printed. *'Balfour
Family in Ruins* was quite a juicy one.'

'Stop pretending you don't care.'

'I shouldn't care. I've had it for most of my life.
I've been the "bad twin" since I was packed off to
boarding school. I even lived up to the nickname
the press gave me.'

He gave a sardonic smile. 'Did it work?'

'Did what work?'

'The attention-seeking behaviour?'

'No. To get attention, there has to be someone
around to give you attention.' Bella sniffed. 'My
mother died, stepmother number one dumped me
in boarding school and left me to fend for myself
and then a few months ago—' she swallowed
'—my second stepmother, Lillian, died. I didn't
spend much time with her but she was a good
person. And she didn't deserve my father. So
you can see that it's pretty hard being saintly in
our family, with him as an example. And pretty
hard being told to mend your ways by someone
like him.' She tried to pull away but Zafiq was
still holding her firmly, his eyes fixed on hers
as he prised the truth from her.

'Are you telling me he sent you alone to the Retreat just after discovering that your sister was the child of another man and that your mother had an affair?'

'I was supposed to think about my behaviour and memorise my Balfour rule. Dignity—' She imitated her father's voice perfectly. '"A Balfour must strive never to bring the family name into disrepute through unbecoming conduct, criminal activity or disrespectful attitudes towards others."'

'You are supposed to follow that rule?'

'Until I stole Amira I've never indulged in criminal activity,' Bella muttered, 'but I guess I've pretty much ticked all the boxes now. Still, I've made the newspapers a fortune.'

'Your father was wrong to send you away with no support.'

Bella's eyes burned but she felt a stab of guilt. 'Actually, it was my fault,' she whispered. 'I behaved horribly.'

Zafiq curved his hands over her shoulders and she shivered because it felt so good to be touched by him.

Too good...

'It was the afternoon before the ball.' Anticipating rejection, Bella pulled away from him, rubbing her fingers over her face to clear the tears. 'My father holds this charity ball every year, you know the sort of thing—glitz and glamour. Anyway, Olivia and I decided to go through our mother's things. There were boxes of books, jewellery, ball gowns—I found a diary.' She dug a tissue out of her pocket and blew her nose. *Who would have thought he was capable of being such a good listener?* 'Being stupid, we read the diary.'

'That's how you discovered your mother's affair?'

'Yes. And immediately it all made sense. I was always proud that I looked like my mother. It was as if there was that special link between us—as if when I looked in the mirror, I was seeing a bit of her reflected there.' Bella fiddled with a strand of her blonde hair. 'But suddenly I discovered why my father can't even bear to look at me. Every time he looks at me, he thinks of her betrayal.'

Zafiq inhaled sharply. 'Bella—'

'Well, obviously it wasn't a great thing to find out. I wanted to keep the whole thing a secret—I didn't want to tell anyone. Especially not Zoe— that's my sister. I thought that would be a hideous, horrible thing to discover about yourself.' She pushed the tissue back into her pocket. 'Why stir up stuff that no one needs to hear?'

'But your twin disagreed?'

'Morally upstanding Olivia—always has to do the "right thing" even when the right thing is going to create carnage. You'd get on well with her. She's big on duty and responsibility. Goes without saying we're non-identical. Anyway, we had a terrible row.' She rubbed her fingers across her forehead. 'Olivia said we should tell Zoe the truth. I pointed out that telling Zoe meant telling *everyone*—I mean, our mother kept it a secret, I wasn't sure it was our business to blurt it all out. You have no idea what a mess it was. Olivia said I was like our mother—' the breath hitched in her throat, remembering just how badly that accusation had hurt her '—and I...I slapped her.'

'You hit your sister?'

'Shocking, isn't it?' Bella whispered, lifting her hand to her mouth. 'I even shocked myself with that one. I've wanted to call her but I don't know if she'll even speak to me.'

Zafiq sighed. 'You were upset, Bella—'

'That's no excuse. Basically, I blew it. And the worst of it was, some paparazzi low life had wormed his way into the party and was standing outside the door. So the next day it was all over the tabloids, and that's how Zoe found out.' The guilt was like a heavy weight, crushing her, and her hands were shaking as she forced herself to confront the issues she'd been avoiding for weeks. 'I didn't want her to know at all, and in the end she found out in the worst possible way. Because of me. I'll never forgive myself for that.'

'It wasn't your fault that the press had gained access to a private party—'

'It *was* my fault.' The tears scalded her throat. 'I know what the press are like. Better than anyone. They've followed me since I was a child. If I'd been more guarded—but I'm not. I find it impossible not to just say what I'm thinking and I gave them what they wanted. I gave them the shots and I gave them the stories. And this was the story of the decade. My father thought I'd done it on purpose for the attention. That's why he banished me.'

'Did it occur to you that your father might have sent you to the Retreat to protect you?'

Bella gave a bitter laugh. 'No. He sent me there to punish me. He knew that being on my own with my guilt would be the very worst thing. If I'd stayed at home I would have partied, got drunk— just tried to forget about it. He forced me into a position where I had no choice but to think about what I'd done. And I deserved it.'

'You're *extremely* hard on yourself. You found

yourself in a situation that no one would have found easy.'

'Olivia thought it was black and white.'

'Life is never black and white.'

'Especially not in the desert. It's all red and gold.' Trying to lighten the atmosphere, Bella wiped her cheek with the palm of her hand. 'Do you know the funny thing? I've actually grown to love it here. I love the fact there are no press. I love the fact that people aren't bugging me to attend their parties just so they get in the newspapers.' She blushed. 'That sounds boastful, but honestly, it's what people do. They invite me to places just because they know the press will follow.'

'And you never know who your real friends are.'

'I guess you know that feeling.' She looked down at herself, noticing the splash of mud on her cream jodhpurs. Even without a mirror she knew she must look a mess. 'Do you realise how great it has been to know that I can muck out a horse and appear all hot and sweaty without having to worry about seeing myself on every front page tomorrow?'

'Didn't you like being on the front pages?'

'I suppose I must have done for a while,' Bella

admitted, feeling her cheeks redden. 'To start with, I liked the attention. I felt as though people loved me. And then I realised that of course they didn't love me.' She gave a twisted smile because it was hard being that honest with herself, let alone with him. 'They liked watching me slip up. Bad Bella. But I'm not Bad Bella here. I'm *not* corrupting your brother, or your sister, or any of your staff, although I don't blame you for think-ing that—'

'Rachid is half in love with you.'

'Only half?' Bella grinned through her tears. 'I must be losing my touch. Maybe I need to wash my hair more often.'

Suddenly it was all too much for her. He was so, so unbelievably attractive and powerful and confident that she swayed towards him.

I'm like a feeble plant, she thought wildly, *trying to wind myself around a strong stake.*

Consumed by longing, she put out her hand, drawn to him by an invisible force and by feel-ings so intense that she was humbled. Nothing mattered but being close to him. 'I've missed you so much.'

He tensed instantly and his lack of response was more humiliating than anything that had hap-pened to her before.

Aware that she'd just made a bigger fool of herself than ever before, Bella turned her face away. Her cheeks burned with humiliation and she wished she could just slide under the straw and hide.

She withdrew her hand. 'As I was saying,' she croaked, 'I've missed you because I really wanted to tell you how well I've been doing. You'd be really proud of me. I've been helping to train Batal for the race, and—' Once again she almost told him she'd been exercising Batal, but then she decided he'd probably have a meltdown if she told him that so she passed over that bit. 'He's going to do well, I know he is.'

She hoped he'd think he'd misinterpreted her first remark and that appeared to be the case because he relaxed slightly.

'I admit I'm surprised that Hassan can handle him.'

'Oh, Hassan is a good rider,' Bella said glibly, focusing on Amira. 'It's all going to be fine.' She still hadn't got her head around who was actually going to ride Batal in the race itself. 'There's only one more week to go. It's going to feel weird once it's over. No one talks about anything else.'

He didn't want her, she thought numbly. *The one man she really wanted had rejected her.*

'It is an important event in our calendar.' Zafiq stroked Amira gently. 'Have you spoken to your father since you've been here?'

'No. I've been too busy.' She didn't confess that she was nervous of phoning any of her family in case they rejected her.

She was in disgrace, wasn't she?

'What happened to your craving for your laptop, your phone and your iPod?'

Bella patted her pocket. 'iPod here. I listen to music while I'm mucking out the horses. Amira really likes Linkin Park and Muse. Loud music sends Batal into orbit so I tend to listen to Mozart when I'm with him. Sometimes Schubert.'

He gave her a curious look. 'So Bella Balfour really is turning over a new leaf.'

'Looks that way.' Bella held tightly to Amira's mane to stop her reaching out to him.

She had to win the race, she told herself fiercely. There was no one else who could ride Batal. She had to find a way.

For once in her life, she wasn't going to let anyone down.

CHAPTER NINE

'BELLA, you can't ride the stallion in the race! It's too dangerous!'

The jockeys were gathered round her in one corner of the barn, all uneasy about the plan.

'You have a better suggestion?' Bella was squeezing her feet into her boots and trying not to think about Zafiq. Rumour had reached her ears that he'd been on a two-day trip to Europe, ostensibly to meet some 'suitable' princess and Bella had never known such agony. 'I'm the same height as Hassan. Everyone thinks Hassan has been riding Batal—they have no reason to think it's me.'

'They'll notice soon enough when you ride into the winner's enclosure.'

'I've thought about that—' Bella tucked her shirt into the waistband of her jodhpurs. 'Batal isn't going to stop when he finishes the race. I'm going to make sure he keeps galloping. He tries to do it all the time, so no one will guess it's intentional. They'll just think he's being his usual moody self. I'll let him bolt all the way back to the stables. Hassan, you'll be waiting back here in the stables so that when everyone arrives, you're standing here holding the stallion, apologetic that you couldn't hold him back and irritated that you missed the applause and attention.'

Connor, a jockey who had travelled from Ireland to take a job in the Sheikh's world-famous stables, rolled his eyes. 'I don't like it. None of us think that Kamal's fall was an accident. Something spooked Batal. What if they come after you?'

'They can't do much in front of an audience, can they? Not with the Sheikh there watching.' *Would he be with his princess?* Ignoring the sudden spasm of pain in her chest, Bella crammed the hat on her head. 'You lot go ahead. I'm going to appear at the very last moment so no one will have time to get a good look at me. You're going to tell everyone that Batal has been acting up and we don't trust him with the other horses for too long. I'm going to appear about thirty seconds before the race starts and hit the ground running.'

'Let's just hope you don't hit the ground before you reach the finish line,' Hassan said drily, but there was a look of respect in his eyes. 'I really hope you don't get hurt, Bella.'

She was already hurting so badly it felt as though she'd been dragged across the desert behind a horse. The thought of Zafiq laughing and smiling with another woman made her ache....

'Oh, for crying out loud!' Irritated with herself, Bella glanced at her watch. 'Just go, will you? You lot are making me nervous. How long have I got?'

'Everyone has already gone to the starting line. You're sure you know the course?'

'I gallop flat out until I reach the marker, then I turn round and come back.'

'And—'

'And I have to cross the line first or Sheikh Zafiq loses his favourite mare,' Bella snapped. 'Yes, I know that.' And the pressure was getting to her. Everything rested on her and the responsibility made her insides quake.

What if she let everyone down?

That was what she did, wasn't it?

When it really mattered, she always messed up.

What if Batal lost because of her? What if she fell off before the finishing line?

Connor squeezed her shoulder. 'Just ride. Don't look left or right.'

And don't think about Zafiq, Bella told herself,

her courage faltering as she watched them all leave.

Now it was just her and the stallion—and Hassan hovering nervously in the background, ready to help her mount the powerful animal.

It didn't help that Batal was in a foul mood, stamping his feet, showing the whites of his eyes, his head snaking forward to bite anyone who came near.

'Oh, get a grip,' Bella said wearily as she approached the snorting horse. 'There's no reason for you to be tense. You could win this stupid race with your hooves tied together. Just don't let anyone give you a fright. You're the boss, OK? Alpha horsey.'

Hassan gave her a leg up into the saddle and then retreated to a safe distance. 'Are you ready?'

'As ready as I'll ever be.' Bella felt the stallion's muscles ripple and shimmer beneath her, as if he was coiled, ready to spring. Nerves fluttered in her belly. 'I wish there was a seat belt. If you throw me off, we lose Amira,' she reminded the horse and then grinned at Hassan. 'Go and hide behind a hay bale. You're supposed to be the one riding, remember?'

'The whole of Al-Rafid is depending on you,

Bella,' Hassan said hoarsely, and Bella rolled her eyes.

'No pressure, then.' She sat tight as the stallion went up on his hind legs, sawing the air with his legs. 'Here we go. Circus time.' But the moment the stallion hit the ground she drove him forward and knew that she had to keep doing that. It was as if the horse knew what was about to happen and just wanted to get on with it.

She urged him along the track that led directly from the stables to the desert. Even before she arrived at the starting line she could hear the roar of the crowd.

'Is this going to freak you out?'

But for once Batal was behaving himself, his ears flicking backwards and forwards like radar, listening to the cheers.

'Attention seeker.' Bella adjusted the scarf across her face, hoping that it didn't fall. If it did, she was sunk.

Riding up towards the starting line, Connor took the bridle. 'The Sheikh was starting to think you weren't coming. I told him we didn't want Batal to be in a public place any longer than necessary. Oh, no—' His face paled. 'Bella, he's coming across to wish you luck! If he gets too close he's going to know you're not Hassan.'

'Stop him,' Bella said urgently, turning Batal towards the starting line. 'Tell him I've got my hands full, tell him I don't want to tempt fate—tell him *anything*, but don't let him get close to me. How long have I got before the start?'

'One minute.'

It felt like the longest minute of her life.

As Connor hurried away to head off Zafiq, Bella urged the stallion towards the rope, her hands shaking on the reins.

Batal threw up his head and squealed, as if to say, *Who put this idiot on my back?* and Bella gave a weak laugh because she was starting to agree.

And then she caught the vicious glare from one of the jockeys and her mouth dried. *Trouble*, she thought, but she didn't dare speak, or do anything to reveal herself as a woman, so she had no choice but to keep her mouth closed.

Batal shivered with anticipation, and Bella stared straight ahead of her, determined to do this right. The horse could win; she had no doubt about that. Whether she'd still be on his back as he crossed the finishing line was another matter.

The roar of the crowd intensified and then the flag dropped and the horses sprang forward.

Batal flew into the lead and Bella allowed

him to take the front position, knowing that she couldn't risk being bunched by the others in case one of them tried to unseat her.

As the sand flew into her face, all she was aware of was the pounding of hooves and the pounding of her heart. She could hear horses behind her, but Batal's long, effortless stride immediately lengthened the distance between her and the others.

She smiled, feeling a rush of confidence.

'You are fantastic,' she yelled as the wind and the sand flew past her face and the marker appeared in the distance. 'If you win I'll never say anything bad to you again. I'll even let you kick me and bite me. Go on, Batal, *go on*!'

As she turned Batal around the flag and showed him the finishing line, she felt something yank her leg hard.

Taken by surprise Bella clutched at the stallion's mane, but at full gallop there was no chance of recovery and the next moment she was on the ground, the sudden fall jarring her shoulder, her foot still jammed in the stirrup as her body was dragged bumping and twisting behind the horse.

Shards of agony shot through her body and Bella closed her eyes and prepared to die.

And then suddenly she stopped moving.

Squealing with impatience, Batal was looking down at her as if to say, *All you had to do was sit there and you even messed that up.*

Bella registered that she was still alive but the relief was only fleeting because the rest of the horses were thundering down on her.

Throwing his head in the air Batal reared up and Bella squeezed her eyes shut and prepared to die for a second time. It was obvious that the stallion was going to trample her.

When nothing happened, Bella opened one eye and found herself looking up at the belly of the horse.

The stallion had straddled her, his powerful legs forming a protective cage as the other runners raced past.

Choked with emotion and half crying with pain and gratitude, Bella struggled to sit up, but her shoulder was so agonising that it knocked the breath from her body. As the other horses galloped past her she registered the fact that someone had pulled her off deliberately because they didn't want Batal to win. The same person who had landed Kamal in hospital? The same person who had tried to kidnap Amira?

Raw anger acted like an anaesthetic and Bella

tried again to sit upright, this time using Batal's legs as a frame.

The last of the horses had passed her and she knew there was no hope of catching the winner, but she was determined to finish the race.

Furious with whoever it was who had dragged her off the horse, Bella tried to mount but Batal was too big for her and she couldn't use her hand to pull herself up because her shoulder was hurting too badly.

'I'm sorry,' she sobbed. 'I'm really sorry, Batal.' Tears blurred her vision and then, just when she'd given up, Batal gave a snort and dropped down onto his knees next to her.

For a brief second Bella just gaped at him, and then she slid gingerly onto his back and Batal immediately sprang upwards and forwards, not giving her time to retrieve her stirrups.

Her shoulder was killing her, her hands were shaking and bleeding from her fall and she hung onto a clump of his mane and urged him on, knowing it was hopeless, knowing they couldn't possibly win now.

But Batal had other ideas.

Outraged at having been passed by the other horses, he surged forward with such an astonishing burst of speed that it was as if she'd hit a button saying Turbo Boost.

They passed horse after horse and suddenly Bella felt a tiny flicker of hope come to life inside her.

'Now I know why they call it horsepower. Come on, Batal,' she croaked, wincing as her shoulder jarred again, 'faster, faster, you can do this—'

Determined to be in the lead, Batal dug deep inside himself and found the extra speed he needed. Nostrils flaring, the whites of his eyes showing, he thundered over the winning line half a length ahead of the horse and rider who had tried to put them out of the race.

Remembering that she was supposed to gallop him straight back to the stables, Bella tried to turn him, but Batal had ideas of his own.

Ignoring Bella's feeble attempts to control him with one hand, he slowed his pace and cantered straight across to the stand where the Sheikh and all the VIPs were standing watching the race.

'No...please, no—' Dizzy from her fall and feeling decidedly weird, Bella tugged weakly at the reins, trying to turn him, but the stallion gave an angry snort and came to a halt in front of Zafiq. He stood proudly, neck arched, tail held high as if to say, *That's how it's done.*

A smile spreading across his handsome face, Zafiq stepped down from the stand and walked over to them just as Bella felt darkness close in on her vision.

She heard voices far away—*shocked* voices— followed by an almost eerie silence.

Knowing that she was going to faint, Bella clutched at Batal's mane but it was too late.

'I love you,' she muttered as she slid off the horse and plunged into darkness.

Zafiq paced the floor of the modern, well-equipped hospital room, his eyes never moving from the girl on the bed. 'Fetch another doctor,' he ordered. 'I want another opinion.'

Kalif hesitated. 'You have already had five opinions, Your Highness. All the doctors are in agreement. Miss Balfour banged her head in the fall, but the scan has shown no trauma. She has a mild concussion and is now sleeping. Her shoulder was dislocated and she has many bruises but—'

'She fell from Batal at a gallop…' And he'd never forget that moment. Even when he'd thought it was Hassan who was on the floor, his heart had been in his mouth. To discover that it had been Bella—

'It is indeed a miracle that she survived,' Kalif agreed. 'Had Batal not stopped when he did and had he not protected her with his body... It was an astonishing spectacle. People are talking of nothing else. Not only that an animal of his reputation stopped for the girl, but that he then lowered himself so that she could mount. Quite remarkable.'

'I can't believe she rode the stallion.' Zafiq ran his hand over the back of his neck, so tense that he felt as though he were going to explode. 'I can't believe I didn't spot that it was her.'

'She fooled all of us, Your Highness, but perhaps it was for the best. Had you known it was her, you would have stopped her. And then Batal would not have won the race,' Kalif said logically. 'After Kamal was injured, there was no one else to ride him. She is a very brave young woman.'

Staring at her still form, Zafiq felt suddenly cold as he considered what might have happened. 'She is reckless,' he said hoarsely. 'She has always been reckless.'

A noise behind him made him turn and he saw a crowd of anxious faces in the doorway. His brother Rachid was in front and behind him his sister Sahra, Yousif, his Master of Horse, and at least fifteen of the palace staff.

'Is there any news?' Rachid spoke for all of

them and Zafiq made an exasperated sound as he scanned the number of heads in the corridor.

'She is resting!'

'We are all worried. Even Batal is very unsettled,' Yousif fretted. 'He wants to see her.'

'I'd like to see him,' came a small voice from the bed, and they all turned and saw a white-faced Bella, struggling to sit up.

'Don't move,' Zafiq commanded, but she ignored him, pushing her blonde hair away from her face with a hand that was scraped raw from her fall.

'I need to sit up.' She gave him a wary look, as if she sensed trouble, and then glanced over to the doorway where everyone else was gathered.

Watching her face brighten, Zafiq felt something tug deep inside him.

She'd made friends.

'You were magnificent,' Rachid said hoarsely, crossing the room in two strides and pulling her into a hug without waiting for Zafiq's permission. 'What a woman!'

Stunned by how badly he wanted to drag his brother away, Zafiq watched in tense silence as everyone poured into the room, all of them ignoring him, apparently too overwhelmed by the need to check on Bella to care about protocol.

Smothered in fuss and praise, Bella looked faintly uncomfortable and the only thing she said was addressed to Yousif. 'Is Batal all right?'

'He is very proud of himself,' Yousif assured her immediately. 'I think he knows he has achieved something quite extraordinary. No doubt he will be quite unbearable now.'

Bella grinned weakly and flopped back against the pillows. There was a bruise across one cheekbone where she'd fallen and Zafiq knew she must be aching from head to foot. But she didn't utter a word of complaint; she just listened while everyone bombarded her with stories of the reaction of the crowd.

'They all thought you were dead—'

'—reared up, thought he was going to kill you—'

'—formed a cage—'

'—and when the horse knelt down—'

'—the fastest race anyone has ever seen—'

'—such a relationship between horse and rider—'

'At least we kept Amira,' Bella murmured happily and then frowned slightly as her words were greeted by an uncomfortable silence. 'What? We won, didn't we?'

'You won. The rest of it doesn't matter,' Yousif

said quickly, but Bella glanced between him and Zafiq.

'What's going on? What's wrong?'

'You are a woman,' Yousif muttered. 'The officials are saying that Batal must be disqualified because he was ridden by a woman.'

'What?' Her distress visible, Bella shot upright again, wincing with pain. 'No, they can't do that.' She turned to Zafiq, her expression desperate. 'You're the Sheikh! Tell them they can't do that! Batal won. He was a complete champion. It wouldn't have mattered if he'd been ridden by a monkey, he still would have won. Oh, this is all my fault for fainting at the end. I was supposed to ride him to the stable and swap places with Hassan.' With a groan she covered her face with her hands and Rachid pulled her into his arms.

Seeing her clinging to his brother for comfort was the final straw.

'Out,' Zafiq commanded in a low, dangerous tone. 'All of you out. Bella doesn't need this level of stress.'

But Bella was already struggling out of bed, her legs buckling as her feet touched the floor. 'You can't let them take Amira, Zafiq! Promise me!'

He caught her before she fell and lifted her back onto the bed. Letting her go was harder and he kept his arms around her for a moment, his body tightening as he felt the softness of her skin and the familiarity of her slender frame.

An intensely disciplined man, it exasperated Zafiq that all he wanted to do was flatten her to the bed and soothe her injuries personally. Apart from that one brief kiss in his stables, he hadn't touched her since the desert.

'Zafiq, you have to do something!' Her fingers dug into his arm, her eyes a deep, fierce blue as she pleaded with him. 'Batal won that race!'

Realising that they still had an audience, Zafiq threw a fulminating glance towards the doorway and intercepted his brother's startled gaze. Whether the shock in his eyes was caused by Bella's lack of formality or the fact that Zafiq was still holding her, he had no idea, but that glance was sufficient to ensure their privacy and Rachid coloured and ushered everyone out of the room, leaving the two of them alone.

With a huge effort of will, Zafiq forced himself to release Bella. Sitting down on the edge of the bed he put a safe distance between them but the strain on his self-control combined with the anxiety of seeing her fall, added to his stress levels.

'Once again you were reckless, wilful—' His restraint snapping, he leant forward and kissed her, the softness of her mouth creating an explosion of sensation through his body. After weeks of self-denial he was on the verge of losing control and it was only her sudden gasp that made him draw back. 'I am hurting you,' he groaned guiltily. 'You are bruised everywhere.'

'No, it isn't that—I don't care about that.' Her eyes were swimming with tears. 'I wasn't trying to be wilful or reckless. For once in my life I was trying to do the right thing. There was no one else who could ride him and we all wanted to save Amira—and I messed it up.'

'You didn't mess it up.' Telling himself that it was perfectly reasonable to comfort her or she might make herself worse, Zafiq shifted position and lay down next to her, pulling her carefully into his arms. 'You were ridiculously brave. Do you have any idea how I felt when I saw that it was you? And then when you slid off the horse a second time—'

'You caught me. It's becoming a habit.' Her face rested on his shoulder, her voice muffled.

'That is one habit I would gladly break.' Zafiq moved onto his side so that he could see her properly. 'You are the bravest woman I have ever met.'

'And the most annoying.'

Zafiq gave a faint smile. 'That too.'

'What can you do about Amira?'

'Do you really think I would let them take Amira?'

'But if the rules say a woman can't be riding—'

'The rules don't say that. There is actually no mention of women in the rules. It is time I rewrote them.' Confident that this announcement would ensure an appropriate degree of gratitude, Zafiq was surprised when she pulled away.

'But that won't protect Amira! They've already tried to steal her once, and Kamal's fall wasn't an accident and then there was today…'

A red mist of anger descended on Zafiq's brain as he saw the bluish tinge on her cheek. 'Today,' he said thickly, 'you could have been killed. And the culprit is already in custody. There will be a full investigation but you can trust me when I say that there will be no more attempts to infiltrate my stables.'

'Life's hard, isn't it? You think people are basically good,' she mumbled, 'and then this happens and you realise that some people are horrid.'

'What happened to you was a symptom of greed and jealousy. The horse who came second is owned by the ruler of a neighbouring state, but it was his jockey who pulled you off Batal at the marker.' The thought of what might have happened turned him cold. 'You could have been killed. If the stallion hadn't stopped—'

'I didn't realise you were watching. I thought we were too far away for anyone to see what happened.'

'I had binoculars. And there were officials positioned at every part of the course. They saw what he did. They would have helped you, but you were back on the stallion before they could reach you.' Zafiq drew in a long breath. 'Did you not think that getting back on the horse was dangerous after that fall?'

'I wasn't thinking at all. All I was thinking of was not losing Amira and not letting you and everyone else down. But when I felt his hand on my leg, I thought that was going to be the end of me. With Batal galloping and my foot stuck in the stirrup—and then he just stopped. As if he knew.'

'It was the most surprising, moving thing that anyone watching had ever witnessed. All the more surprising when you know what a bad-tempered, aggressive animal Batal can be. That he showed such gentleness towards you...'

'It's because of him I'm alive,' Bella said simply,

her eyes drifting shut. 'I suppose next time he bites me in the stable, I'll just have to put up with it.'

'You will not be returning to the stable, *habibiti*.' His mind made up, Zafiq delivered the news he knew would bring a smile to her face.

Her eyes flew open and the look on her face was one of horror. 'You're firing me?'

'I am not firing you. You can spend as much time in the stable as you like, but the rest of the time you will be living in the palace,' Zafiq announced, pleased with his solution to the problem.

She would live with him. Why not?

'L-living in the palace?'

'Yes. I have…' Zafiq hesitated and her eyes widened.

'What?'

'I have…missed you.' He found it almost embarrassing to acknowledge just how badly he wanted this woman. 'I've missed having someone who… challenges me.'

'Zafiq—'

'We are not going to talk about this now.' Zafiq sprang to his feet and pressed the buzzer by the bed. 'You are to stay in hospital and rest until at least six doctors agree that you are well enough to return to the palace. Then you will be guest of honour at the winner's banquet.'

She looked slightly dazed. '*Six* doctors?'

'Just to be sure that they know what they're talking about,' Zafiq said firmly. 'I don't want you being discharged and then collapsing again. The winner's banquet is normally held the night of the race but, given what has happened today, I have given instructions for it to be postponed until you are well enough to attend. It is *the* social event of the Al-Rafid calendar. No more sand in your hair, no more improvised tunics and belts made from the leaves of the date palm. An excuse to dress up and party, which is something I'm sure you've been missing out here in the desert.'

'You don't like me with sand in my hair?'

He was so relieved to hear her sounding like herself that he smiled. 'It's time you were Bella Balfour again. And this time you will be standing by my side, *habibiti.*'

So what exactly did all this mean?

You will be standing by my side…

Did he mean by his side for one official banquet? By his side for a whole night? *Lots of nights?*

She'd been waiting for him to mention the fact

she'd said, 'I love you,' when she fell off Batal, but he'd avoided the topic.

Bella stared at the delicate rose petals floating on the surface of the enormous bath, unable to contain the excitement fizzing inside her even though she knew their relationship had no future.

He'd been to see his princess, hadn't he? He was already considering marriage.

'You are very quiet, madam,' one of the women said, and she gave a small smile, pushing away that thought. She was here now. That was what counted.

'Just thinking. You have no idea how long it is since I wallowed in a bath.' It had been weeks. First she'd been in the desert with the Sheikh and then she'd been living in the stables and was always far too tired to take anything more than a quick shower.

She was woman enough to be excited at the prospect of walking into the room and watching Zafiq's face when he saw her wearing a dress.

Running her hand through the scented water, Bella suddenly found herself thinking about the swims they'd shared in the cooling waters of the oasis.

Feeling a sudden pang, she frowned. This was

much better, she told herself firmly. It didn't even compare.

She sat still while the team of women washed her hair and combed soothing, conditioning oils through each golden strand.

'The whole country is talking about the way you rode the devil horse. It is no wonder that His Highness is so taken with you.' One of the women rubbed oil into Bella's shoulders. 'You are brave as well as beautiful.'

'I feel as though I'm being prepared for the harem,' Bella muttered and then wished she'd kept her mouth shut when the women exchanged shocked glances. 'Look…sorry, just ignore my big mouth.'

'It is very unusual for the Sheikh to have such a public relationship with a woman,' another of the women said quietly. 'Since the death of his father he is a man whose sole focus has been his duty.'

'Yeah, I know.' Bella leant her head back against the bath and closed her eyes. 'To him emotions and love are a sign of weakness—blah, blah—I've heard it all before.' It had been impossible not to hear some of the gossip that had hummed around the stables and the more she'd heard, the more surprised she'd been that he'd ever embarked on a relationship with her. Even though their's had been a secret desert tryst, it was obvious to her that his own strict code of behaviour should have prevented him from succumbing to the chemistry that had connected the two of them.

'He is afraid of being like his father,' the woman said in a soft voice. 'Sheikh Zafiq's father was a good man, but he had no self-control when it came to women. The woman he married. She was—'

'A mistake,' her friend said grimly, rinsing the oil from Bella's hair. 'She thought only of herself. Everything she demanded, he bought her. She was wilful and extravagant and had no sense of duty.'

Bella blushed, knowing that some of that description could have been applied to her up until a short time ago. 'I bet you don't want to see him with anyone like her, then.'

'You are nothing like her, madam.' The women helped her out of the bath, wrapped her in soft, warm towels and started to dry her hair methodically. 'Everyone in Al-Rafid is pleased to see the Sheikh smiling. These past few years have been difficult for him. Not only did he become ruler at a young age, but he had responsibility for his younger brothers and sisters. He has had little time to himself and that is not good for such a virile, masculine man.'

And what little time he'd had, she'd ruined, Bella thought guiltily, talk of Zafiq's virility sending an excited shiver down her spine. She barely noticed as the women slid a dress over her head and adjusted the straps.

He didn't allow himself to love, did he?

He was afraid that love would make him weak.

Which was why he was planning a formal arrangement with some princess he didn't know.

So what was tonight all about?

Suddenly aware that they were all looking at her expectantly, Bella looked in the mirror and her mouth fell open.

'Oh! That's— You— How—?'

'You are pleased? You have such beautiful, beautiful hair,' one of the women enthused, 'but it was in bad condition from the sand and the sun—'

'And cramming it under a riding hat.' Bella stared in disbelief at her reflection. 'I used to spend hours getting ready for parties, but I've never managed to make myself look like this. What have you done?' Her hair shone with health and her skin glowed. The subtle application of make-up accentuated her best features and her mouth was a tempting, subtle pink that could have passed for nude. 'Clever. It looks as though I'm not wearing make-up.'

'You hardly need make-up now the bruises have faded. And we have merely made the most of what nature has given you, madam. You are truly stunning. And Sheikh Zafiq is going to be pleased.'

Pleased.

As if she were some sort of gift, ready for him to unwrap.

Bella frowned at that thought and then pushed it away. No. She wasn't going to diminish this. The fact that he'd invited her to the formal dinner as his guest was an enormously big deal. It showed that he cared about her.

She *knew* he cared about her. Why else would he have arranged for six doctors to check on her condition before allowing her to be discharged? Why else would he have moved her into the most ornate wing of his palace and bought her all these beautiful clothes?

After a month without him, a month during which she'd filled every waking minute with work in order to distract herself from the pain of not seeing him, Bella could hardly breathe with excitement.

She just had to get through the dinner, and then they'd be on their own and she'd have his luscious, gorgeous body all to herself.

Sliding her feet into elegant shoes, she walked out of her bedroom suite, following a deferential member of Zafiq's staff along miles of ornate corridor and into a large opulent room where hundreds of eyes turned to look at her.

Instantly everyone rose to their feet as a sign of respect and Bella flushed scarlet.

'Gosh—this is embarrassing.'

'They are all thanking you.' Zafiq was by her side, pulling her arm through his and leading her to the head of the table.

Bella shrank as everyone started to clap. 'They're clapping because I fell off a horse?'

'They're clapping because you put your life at risk for Al-Rafid. Amira is something of a national treasure, as I have explained to you. It is because of you that she is still with us. They are already celebrating future Derby winners.'

'Batal was certainly giving her flirtatious looks this afternoon.' Bella smiled awkwardly at everyone who was watching. 'I think he's hoping he might get lucky tonight.'

'Not just Batal.' Zafiq's gaze lingered on her face. 'You look beautiful.'

'I'm glad you think so after all the effort those poor women put into making me presentable.' In the past, dressing up had given her confidence but now Bella felt a thousand times more awkward than she had in the desert.

Why? She was used to huge, public gatherings and yet she felt as shy and conspicuous as she had at her first ball at Balfour Manor.

Sitting down next to him it was impossible not to be aware that she was the focus of attention. 'They're wondering what a guy like you is doing with a girl like me.'

'I think it's obvious to every red-blooded man in the room what I'm doing with you,' Zafiq drawled, apparently indifferent to the gossip and speculation. 'If it weren't for protocol we would have skipped this part of the evening and gone straight up to my rooms.'

'Wow. I must fall off your horse more often.' Bella kept her tone light, but her heart was thundering like Batal's hooves in the race. *So it wasn't going to end with dinner, then.*

Unable to eat anything, she pushed her food around her plate. Every time Zafiq's arm brushed against hers she jumped, and every time he turned to talk to her she found herself tongue-tied and gauche.

By the time he finally rose from the table and led her from the room, she was a nervous wreck. The only thing she knew for sure was that she was crazily in love with him.

She had no idea at all how he felt about her.

Grateful, obviously, because she'd saved his beloved Amira. But was it anything more than that?

As Zafiq guided her past the guards and into his private room, Bella caught his arm. 'Wait a minute. I really need to ask you something.'

'Anything.' His tone indulgent, he removed his tie and stepped towards her, cupping her face in his hands. 'But make it quick. I've already waited too long for this moment and I'm not prepared to waste what time we have together talking.'

'Would you have invited me as your guest to the ball if I'd lost the race?'

'What sort of a question is that?'

'I—I just want to understand why I'm here.' *Say something nice to me*, her brain was shrieking and he gave a smile of masculine appreciation.

'You're here,' he said huskily, 'because I have denied myself long enough.'

'So what's happened to duty and responsibility?'

'Our relationship has no impact on my ability to perform my duties.' He slid his fingers
through her hair and trailed his lips along the
line of her jaw and Bella moaned, feeling the
immediate response of her body.

Suddenly she was on fire—his weeks of denial
had been her weeks of denial, too. And during
those weeks she'd thought long and hard about
who she was and who she wanted to be.

'Wait a minute.' She pulled back slightly, remembering the promise she'd made to herself in
the cold, dark hours of the night when she'd lain
awake feeling lonely and reliving those moments
in the desert.

She was going to change.

She'd promised herself that if fate ever threw
him in her path again, she wasn't going to just
follow her instincts, she was going to use her
brain.

If he'd wanted her for anything other than sex,
then it would have been different, but now she
was here, she was under no illusions about what
was on offer.

'I *can't* wait.' His hand came behind her neck
and his mouth came down on hers, his kiss dark,

forbidden and meltingly sexy, and a bolt of heat shot through her from mouth to toes. Only the memory of the emotional agony she'd suffered over the past few weeks gave her the strength to do what she had to do.

'No! This isn't— I can't!' She pushed against his chest. 'I don't want to be the one you have fun with while you're finalising plans to choose your bride and do your duty.'

'You're saying you don't want this?'

'Of course I want this.' Bella groaned. 'I just don't want what's coming afterwards. I don't want to have to drag myself out of bed every morning feeling as though the world has ended. I don't want that awful ache in my chest. I felt bruised, Zafiq, like you'd gouged part of me away with a blunt instrument—it was worse than falling off Batal. I just don't want to feel that way again.'

'You're saying no?' Under different circumstances the disbelief in his tone would have made her laugh.

'I know that isn't a word you've heard very often, but if you look it up in the dictionary, it's the opposite of yes. And I'm not saying no because I want to challenge your authority or be generally annoying, or do any of those things

likely to make you want to overrule me on prin-
ciple. I'm just trying to keep us both sane.'

'Saying no keeps you sane?'

'Yes…no.' Bella groaned and dug her fingers
in her hair, gritting her teeth with frustration. 'I
can't have an on-off relationship. It's like rubbing yourself over the teeth of a saw! It hurts too
much.'

The breath hissed through his teeth. 'Staying
away from you has been driving me mad.'

'So why did you stay away from me, Zafiq?
Was it because of your father?' She was taking
a huge risk, but she had to ask the question. 'Are
you trying not to be like him? Is that why you're
denying what we have?'

'What do you know about my father?'

'I know you're afraid to be like him. I know
you'll marry someone you've chosen with your
head, not your heart. And—' it took a supreme
effort to force the words past her lips '—I don't
want what you're offering. I don't want to be the
Sheikh's mistress!' Wrestling her self-control
back into some sort of shape, she stepped back
from him.

His hands moved and, for a moment, she
thought he was going to reach for her and haul

her against him, but then he stepped back too, his eyes wary.

'You're saying that you don't want what we had in the desert?'

'That was different,' Bella whispered, pressing her fingers to her throat. 'We were a million miles from our real lives. For a time we both escaped from who we really are. It was just the two of us.'

'It is still just the two of us.'

'No. You're still the ruler of Al-Rafid, Zafiq. Do you think I don't know how hard you've been struggling *not* to renew our relationship? That night when you came down to the stables to accuse me of sleeping with Rachid—'

'That was *not* my finest hour.'

'Don't apologise. Honestly, we're past that. I don't even blame you for thinking it, given everything the newspapers have written about me. But that night taught me that, to you, I'm a temptation that has to be resisted at all costs.'

'If that were true, you would not be here now.'

'Really?' She gave a lopsided smile. 'Do you know what I think? I think even you aren't quite as strong as you'd like to think you are. I think our chemistry is pretty hot and it would be all too easy to let it take over and for us to think, *What the heck—let's just have a good time and enjoy ourselves while we can.* But there's always a price for living in the moment.'

'You are speaking from experience...'

'Yes. And for once I've learned from that experience. I know you, Zafiq. You might be able to leave behind duty and responsibility for one steamy night, but you won't leave it behind for long. It's who you are. You're a brilliant ruler and your people love you. They *need* you. And when the time comes you'll choose a suitable woman to be by your side to give you children and all those other respectable, duty-like things.' Bella swallowed hard. 'And that isn't going to be me, is it?'

There was a lengthy, protracted silence.

He took so long to reply that hope flickered to life in her heart.

Hoping desperately that she was wrong about him, she reached out her hand but he simply stared at it for a moment, a muscle working in his jaw. And then he looked her in the eyes.

'I will not make the same mistakes in my marriage that my father made in his.'

It was like being stabbed through the heart and she pulled her hand back and rubbed it against her chest, trying to ease the pain. 'Then this is goodbye, Zafiq.'

'Wait! I haven't finished.'

'But I have.' Bella ignored his command, her hand on the door handle. 'Honestly, Zafiq, this is *so* hard—you have no idea how hard, especially for someone like me. I don't do this, OK? I don't behave for the greater good, nor do I act unselfishly, so you've got to give me some help here! It's—it's like tipping away a drink when you're an alcoholic, or saying no to chocolate when you're starving.'

'I'm an addictive substance?'

She was embarrassed she'd revealed so much about her feelings for him. 'We're not good for each other! Why did you even invite me tonight? I was doing OK in your stables.' Sort of.

'You're saying you would have preferred to continue working in my stables?'

'In a way, yes,' she said miserably. 'I did it to prove to everyone that I wasn't Bad Bella, that I could be responsible. But I'd forgotten how much I love horses. And I've discovered that I love the responsibility. I love knowing I managed to win that race—well, Batal won it, I know, but I was on his back and I'm proud of that. It felt as though I'd achieved something.'

'You achieved a great deal, and…I want you more than I've ever wanted any other woman.'

Sensing his struggle, Bella stared at him with a lump in her throat. *Hug me*, she thought to herself. *Drag me into your arms and tell me you can't live without me.*

But he stood rigid, as if he were hanging onto control by a thread. 'I have never offered another woman what I'm offering you now. I'm inviting you to live in the palace with me.'

'As your mistress. I don't want that, Zafiq. You treated me to dinner because I won the race, but that's over now. And now I'm going back to the stables.' Her knees were shaking, her stomach was quivering and every nerve in her body was straining to touch him. She'd never, *ever* in her life wanted anything or anyone as badly as she wanted him and denying herself was the hardest thing she'd ever done.

Seeing his handsome features frozen in a mask of disbelief, she almost gave in to temptation and launched herself at him, and then she reminded herself that sooner or later he'd dump her.

And if life had taught her anything, it was that she didn't want to be with a man who didn't love her.

'Thanks for this evening, Zafiq.' Bella opened

the door before she could change her mind, knowing that he wasn't going to say anything with his guards listening to every word. 'And thanks for the bath. You have no idea how good it felt to finally get my hands on a bottle of decent conditioner.'

CHAPTER TEN

RACHID was talking to Yousif when Bella emerged from Amira's box the next morning.

Both of them stared at her as if she were a mirage.

'What?' She snapped the word and then instantly regretted it because both men had been good friends to her. 'Sorry,' she muttered. 'Not enough sleep last night.' Then she realised how they'd interpret that remark and blushed. 'I mean, because I still ache all over and, no matter how I lie, I can't sleep. I'm going to have words with Batal.'

'You can't.' Yousif gave her a strange look. 'His Highness has driven to the State of Zamira. He has taken Batal with him.'

Bella removed a piece of straw that was clinging to her hair. 'Well, I'll have words with him when he returns. Big, macho brute.'

Rachid paled. 'Zafiq hurt you?'

'Not Zafiq, I was talking about Batal.' Bella frowned at them. 'I fell off his back, remember?

And he's a long way from the ground. It felt like falling from the top of the Empire State Building.'

The two men exchanged looks. 'His Highness did not say when he would be returning,' Yousif said in a strangled voice. 'This was an unscheduled trip. He has gone to visit Princess Yasmina, the woman everyone is hoping he will marry.'

Bella felt as though she'd fallen off the horse again. Every single part of her ached. 'Right. Well…' She gave a twisted smile. 'I have things to do. I'm taking Amira for a ride. On my own.'

'But if you are still bruised from your fall—'

'Kill or cure.' Bella strolled back to the stable, her mind in a mess. After their conversation the night before, he'd gone to meet his future wife. Why did that hurt so much when she'd always known that was what he'd do?

Leaning her head against Amira, she closed her eyes.

Because she hadn't expected him to do it quite so quickly.

Regret stabbed her hard in the ribs. Perhaps she should have taken what he'd offered the night before. She should have had that one last night together.

Reminding herself that one more night would

have intensified the pain rather than lessen it, she saddled Amira and led her into the yard. She climbed stiffly onto the mounting block, grimacing slightly as every muscle in her body shrieked a protest.

She didn't even know where she was going.

All she knew was that she wanted to be on her own for a while in the desert.

Bella gave a humourless laugh. 'That bang on the head must have got to me,' she told the mare, urging her forward out of the yard. 'Two months ago I would have sold the contents of my wardrobe to escape from all that sand. Now, not only do I not have a wardrobe to sell, but I don't even care, and I can't think of anything more relaxing than riding in the desert. Do you think I need help?'

Amira gave a whinny and broke into a trot, but Bella reined her in with a groan.

'No, no. That's too bumpy. I feel as though I'm in cocktail shaker. Do you mind just walking?'

The horse didn't seem to object, or maybe she sensed Bella's fragile state because she walked carefully, picking her way over rough surfaces until she reached the sandy track that led into the desert.

A lizard scuttled across their path and Bella

watched it with a lump in her throat, remembering the nights she and Zafiq had spent together
staring up at the stars.

Talking. Laughing. Making love.

Was that why she was riding into the desert?

To torture herself with memories?

She'd grown to love the narrow, dusty streets
of Al-Rafid with its colourful souks and high
stone walls. She'd grown to love the stables and
the friends she'd made. But most of all she loved
Zafiq, in a way she hadn't known it was possible
to love another person. She wanted what was best
for him and she could see that wasn't her.

But could she carry on living here, and watch
him marry? Could she watch him smile at another woman and lift another woman's child in
his arms?

'It would be like falling on a cactus,' she muttered to Amira, 'and then getting up and doing it
again. I'm not that much of a masochist. It would
be easier to recover away from him.'

It wasn't as if she didn't have money now. Her
father had cut off her allowance, but she didn't
need an allowance any more, did she? Zafiq paid
his staff well and she'd been working too hard to
spend any of the money she'd earned. As a result

she had more than enough for a flight back to England.

Perhaps she'd go back to Balfour Manor and make her peace with her father. Then she'd go and get a job in a racing stable. Or maybe an eventing yard. Somewhere she could be part of a team and make a difference.

If she worked hard enough she wouldn't have time to think about how much she was hurting inside.

Zafiq returned from the desert to find everyone in the stables electrified with anxiety.

'Bella has not returned,' Rachid reported as Zafiq led Batal out of the horsebox.

Having thought of nothing but Bella for the past two days, he felt colour streak across his cheeks. 'Returned from where?'

'The desert.' Rachid filled the hay net and retreated to a safe distance from the stallion's hooves. 'She left the same day you did. She's taken Amira into the desert. And the horses miss her. They keep putting their heads over the stable doors and calling for her.'

Feeling as though he was one step behind everyone else, Zafiq struggled to keep his tone patient. 'You let her take Amira into the desert?'

'She didn't tell us where she was going and it was only when she was late arriving back from her ride that we found her note. It's her final trip,' Yousif said dismally. 'She said she needed to go there one more time before she leaves us.'

'She is alone?' Zafiq felt the kind of fear he'd only felt once before—when he'd realised it was Bella on the back of his stallion. 'You didn't try and stop her? Do you have any idea how vulnerable she is out there? She knows nothing about surviving in the desert. Nothing!'

Rachid looked at him. 'Has anyone ever managed to stop Bella doing what she wants? She rode Batal against everyone's advice. She has a mind of her own, Zafiq.'

He knew that.

He knew all about the way Bella's mind worked.

'She is safe,' Yousif said quietly. 'She called us last night from a satellite phone, just to let us know she was OK. All she would say was that she was staying somewhere special. We think she's probably at the Retreat but you know they never divulge the names of their guests. She's probably making the most of her last few days. She said that she will miss us all,' he said gloomily, 'but nowhere near as much as we will miss *her*, Your Highness. She is the best groom I have ever had. How Amira will cope when she leaves, I do not know. I have four vets ready to care for her but I know she will pine dreadfully. The horses love Bella. Even the dogs love her.'

'Everyone loves her,' Rachid said, glancing towards the desert with worry in his eyes. 'Perhaps I made a mistake. Kamal said I should have sent someone to follow her but she was most insistent—'

'Kamal?' Zafiq stared at them with growing frustration. 'What does Kamal have to do with this? He is still in hospital.'

'Bella has visited him every day since he's been in hospital,' Rachid told him. 'Taking him pictures of the horses. She really makes him laugh. She tells terrible jokes.'

Zafiq knew all about her terrible jokes. 'What do you mean, you will all miss her when she leaves—where is she going?'

'Home to England.'

Zafiq felt as though he'd been thumped in the chest. 'Why would she do that?'

'She didn't say. She just said it was the right thing.'

'She should not have gone into the desert!'

Yousif cleared his throat. 'Stopping Bella is a

bit like trying to stop Batal when he is galloping, Your Highness. A lost cause.'

'She will certainly be lost by now,' Zafiq said through gritted teeth, and Yousif flushed.

'You are worried about Amira, of course—what do you want us to do, Your Highness?'

Realising that his concern for Bella eclipsed his worry for his favourite mare, Zafiq dragged his fingers through his hair. They were waiting for him to make a decision and for the first time in his life cool, rational thought evaded him.

Driven by concern for Bella, he vaulted onto the back of his stallion. 'I will ride after her.'

'I will come with you,' Rachid said immediately, but Zafiq shook his head.

'No.'

Yousif and Rachid looked at each other. 'At least take your guards. Do you want us to call the Retreat and say you are on your way?'

'No guards. And I don't want you to contact the Retreat.' Zafiq knew she wouldn't be there. At the thought of her sitting cross-legged, drinking herbal tea, he almost laughed. But his desire to laugh faded as he thought about how much danger she was in.

She thought she knew the desert…

And he knew that an assumption of knowledge

could be more dangerous than an admission of ignorance. It was impossible not to think about what had happened last time Bella had ridden into the desert alone.

Nursing a clear memory of her lying in the sand, dangerously dehydrated, Zafiq urged Batal forwards and prayed that he wouldn't be too late.

Bella was lying on her back in the pool when she heard the thunder of hooves and saw the growing cloud of sand. 'Our peace is over, Amira.'

But her heart sank because she knew who was coming.

Would he arrest her for stealing his horse a second time?

Amira threw up her head and whinnied, her ears flicking forwards and her nostrils flaring.

Deciding that she didn't have time to grab her clothes, Bella stood so that just her head appeared above the water as Zafiq rode into the camp like a warrior going into battle.

Watching him, Bella wondered whether the pain would fade once she was thousands of miles away from him. 'What happened to the princess,' she called lazily, hiding her agony behind indifference, 'not pretty enough? Or did she answer you back?' She skimmed her hands over the water and watched as the ripples spread across the surface.

'Even after weeks in my country you have developed no respect for the harshness of the desert.' His voice a furious growl, Zafiq sprang from the horse with an athletic grace that Bella found it impossible not to admire.

'Calm down. You're sheikhing yourself up over nothing.'

He cast her a warning glance and walked across to Amira. 'Has the mare had water?'

'No, I'm watching her slowly die of thirst.' Bella wondered how long it would take her to drive him away in a temper. Not long, she hoped, because every word, every look, was killing her. 'Of *course* she's had water. You really think I'm stupid, don't you?'

His eyes were on hers. 'No,' he said slowly, his accent thickening the words. '*Not* stupid. I think you are a very bright, very misunderstood woman.'

Taken aback, Bella stared at him. 'Oh, well… in that case, I'm happy to tell you that I've fed her, given her water, kept her in the shade and kept a watch for snakes and scorpions like you taught me. I even slept next to her with a dagger last night, just in case. Did I miss anything?'

Zafiq's gaze scanned the horse. 'She looks well.'

'Good. What are you doing here anyway?'

'I've come to tell you that I'm getting married.'

Bella felt as though he'd punched her. 'You came all the way out here to deliver that news in person?' She wanted to howl with pain. 'That was thoughtful of you.'

'You need to know.'

Typical man, Bella thought miserably. Practical to the last. 'OK, well, now I know, so you can go away again and leave me in peace.'

'You are coming back with me.'

'No!' Bella bit her lip, too distressed to conjure up a flippant remark. 'Please, Zafiq. I love it here so much. Let me have one more day. I promise I won't let any harm come to Amira. I carried her food, I have loads of water—I thought it through, honestly.' She was ready to beg, but his hard, handsome face showed no sign of softening.

'I need you back in Al-Rafid.'

'That's completely unfair!' She didn't bother with formality. 'What is it you want from me? A wedding present? You want me to buy you a bundle of towels and a toaster?' Then she realised how ungracious she was being and blinked away the tears rapidly, cross with herself. 'I wish you well,' she said huskily. 'I really, really hope you'll be very happy. I mean that. I want this marriage to work for you and I'm sure it will because you have a way of making things turn out the way you want them to. I just can't be there to see it happen. And you can't expect that of me.'

'I do expect it. And you *will* be there.'

Bella glared at him, wondering if he had any clue how she felt about him. 'Are you dense or something?'

His head flicked back and shock flared in his dark eyes. 'Are you calling me dense?'

'Well, you're either dense or monumentally insensitive and neither attribute is exactly something to boast about,' Bella snapped, pushing aside a strand of weed that wound itself round her wrist. 'If you can't think about my feelings, at least think about your wife. How would she feel?'

'I hope she will feel proud to be standing by my side.'

'Well, I'm sure she will. And I certainly don't want to spoil her day by being in the audience. Ex-girlfriends anonymous. Oh, go away, Zafiq! Go and torture someone else.' Feeling the lump grow in her throat, Bella turned away and concentrated on the date palms that shaded the pool, furious with herself for not being strong enough to go to his wedding. 'I can't do it. I can't be there when you marry.'

'Then we have a problem, *habibiti*,' he said softly, 'because I cannot marry without you there.'

Tears blurred her vision. 'Why?'

'Because you are the woman I will be marrying.'

Bella heard the words from far away. She opened her mouth to speak, but no sound came out, and Amira threw up her head and gave a whinny, sensing the change in the atmosphere.

'Get out of the water, Bella!' His voice roughened by exasperation, Zafiq paced to the edge of the pool. 'Say something!'

He looked sensational with the sun turning his hair blue-black, the intensity of his gaze demanding that she look at him.

Shock turned to happiness and then faded away into the most agonising misery.

How could she?

'That's a heck of a sacrifice to make for sex, Zafiq.'

'You think I'm asking you to marry me so that I can have sex?'

'You haven't actually asked me to marry you—' Bella felt something brush against her ankle and gave a squeal. 'Zafiq, there's something in this pool. Ugh!'

He lifted an eyebrow. 'I thought desert creatures didn't bother you?'

'I like lizards but this was slimy.' She was hopping around on one leg, whimpering, and Zafiq gave a masculine smile, stripped off his clothes and joined her in the water in a smooth dive.

He surfaced right next to her and lifted her into his arms. 'It is a piece of weed.'

'What?'

'Around your ankle.' Casually he flipped it away. 'Not a creature. Not slimy.'

'It felt slimy. Put me down, Zafiq—I don't have any clothes on.'

'That's the way I prefer you,' he drawled softly, his eyes on her mouth as he lowered her into the water and drew her against him.

Bella gasped as she felt the heat of his body against hers. 'What are you doing?'

'I'm proposing.' He murmured the words against her mouth. 'Could you say yes quickly so that we can cut straight to the exciting part?'

Mesmerised by the wicked look in his eyes and by the explosive reaction of her own body,

Bella moaned. 'No…I can't— No.' She had to be strong about this. She had to remember what she'd learned—how she was determined to live her life. 'No, Zafiq.'

Zafiq sighed. 'Now what?'

'I said no.'

'I heard you—what I want to know is why. I know you love me, so don't try and deny it.'

'Yes, I do love you. But *you* don't love *me*. And that isn't good enough for me. I don't want to marry for money or status. I don't even want to marry because I'm in love. I'll only marry when it's an equal partnership. When love is given and returned. When we both want the same things. When we're a team because we have an emotional bond, not a paper one.'

'Bella—'

'Whatever anyone says, I'm not like my mother,' Bella whispered. 'I won't marry without love. You taught me how it's possible to feel, and I don't want to feel less than that. And I want a man who feels the same way about me, otherwise what chance will we have? I won't settle for less than a love match because I've seen what happens when you do.'

His dark eyes were locked on hers. 'What makes you think I don't love you?'

'Er, possibly the fact that you've never said those words to me?'

'You have never said those words to me either.'

'I have,' she said hotly. 'When I fell off Batal into your arms, I said, "I love you." And you never mentioned it. You never reacted.'

Zafiq let out a long, exasperated breath. 'I assumed you were talking to the horse.'

'You thought I was declaring my love for your *horse*?'

'You are always saying things like that to the horses. The staff tell me you chat to them all the time, telling them how much you love them and how good they are.'

Bella blushed. 'Well, that's true, I guess.'

'So you admit that I wasn't likely to realise you were declaring your love for me when you landed in my arms.'

Bella pressed her hand against his chest, her fingers feeling the contours of smooth, hard muscle. 'Are you saying—' She cleared her throat, almost afraid to say the words in case she jinxed it. 'Do you mean that—'

'I love you,' he said quietly 'That's what I'm saying, and yes, I mean it.'

Suddenly she felt light-headed. 'You think love is a weakness.'

'I think the relationship my father had with my stepmother was unbalanced, and yes, that made him weak.' Zafiq frowned. 'I was appalled that he seemed unable to resist her. Watching him succumb to the seductive temptations of that woman was the hardest thing I had ever done. I vowed that I would not make the same mistake.'

'And that's why you were so angry with me when I flirted with you?'

'I was determined not to fall into the same trap.'

'I thought you were arrogant and high-handed.'

He gave a faint smile. 'And now?'

'I still think you're arrogant and high-handed,' Bella whispered, 'but you're pretty cute too, and if you get too bossy I'll just argue back.'

'I'm sure you will.' He groaned, sliding his arms around her hair and hauling her against him. 'I love you, Bella Balfour.'

Bella winced and a stab of insecurity sliced through her happiness. 'That's the difficult part, isn't it? My sister Olivia would be better for you. She's practical and sensible. I called her, by the way…'

'Good. And?'

'She'd been worrying too. She felt guilty about the things she said. We had a good conversation. And I spoke to Zoe in New York—she'd been trying to get hold of me.'

'So all your worries are finished.'

'Not really. How are your people ever going to accept you marrying Bad Bella?'

'My people think you are Brave Bella.' He cupped her face in his hands and kissed her gently on the mouth, his voice vibrating with sincerity. 'To them you are Bold Bella and Beautiful Bella. You are a role model and an inspiration to all who meet you. There is not a bad bone in your body.'

The lump back in her throat, Bella stood still. 'I say the wrong thing—I lose it quite often.'

'I love the fact that you are passionate and honest about your feelings.'

'I've never been anyone's role model before,' she croaked, and he gave a slow smile.

'It's always good to have new experiences in life. All the young girls of Al-Rafid will be watching you, copying you.'

'They'll read awful stuff about me,' Bella mumbled, and he gave a sigh and his mouth tightened.

'We do not censor the press, but nor do we allow the degree of intrusive reporting you have in your country. There will be no journalists climbing the walls of my palace or hiding in the stables.'

'But the past—'

'The past is called the past for a reason. My people care only about what they know and what they see, not about what has been rumoured. They saw a girl willing to put her life on the line for something that mattered to our country.'

'Those stories about me—most of them weren't true,' Bella blurted out, desperate to defend herself for the first time in her life. 'Half the stuff they wrote about me—more than half actually—was all lies. I never had those affairs, but they were determined to write what they wanted so I just let them get on with it. Every time I said hello to a man, it was supposedly a new affair!' Her cheeks burned. 'If I told you there was only ever one man, and that was ages ago, what would you say?'

Zafiq stroked her face with gentle fingers. 'I'd say that he was clearly a fool,' he drawled softly, 'for letting a woman as special as you slip through his fingers.'

'He was the reason I was dropped from the eventing team as a teenager,' Bella confessed. 'I realised that he was just using me and I dumped him, so he spread horrible rumours and the selectors decided I wasn't a good example.'

'I believe you.'

Bella's eyes filled. 'Really? You have no idea how that feels. And being here—' she turned her head, looking at the red-gold sand rising majestically around them '—I feel as if I'm home.'

'You *are* home.'

'I found my way through the desert,' she mumbled. 'You're right that it doesn't all look the same. It isn't just sand. I feel as though this is where I'm meant to be. I want to keep coming here every year. I want to look at the stars and ride through the dunes. I want to make a difference to the people of Al-Rafid—they treat me as if I belong. I feel as though this is the most special place on earth. Just like you do.'

'For me, the most special place on earth is where you are, *habibiti*,' Zafiq said quietly, pulling her into his arms. 'And this is undoubtedly where you are supposed to be. With my people, with my horses, but most of all, with me.'

Her eyes glistening, Bella lifted her face to his, bathing in the truly amazing feeling of being loved for who she was. 'Dignity,' she said, sliding her arms round his neck. 'That's my Balfour rule and I'm going to live up to it, I promise.'

'Dignity has its place, just as long as you don't let it change who you are.' Zafiq lowered his head and Bella smiled.

'I'm yours,' she whispered, and closed her eyes as he kissed her. 'Yours, for ever.'